I0715670

SABOTAGE

NEON
BOOK THREE

ALLYSON LINDT

ACELETTE PRESS

This book is a work of fiction.

While reference might be made to actual historical events or existing locations, the names, characters, places, and incidents are either the product of the author's imagination or are used fictitiously, and any resemblance to actual persons, living or dead, business establishments, events, or locales is entirely coincidental.

Manufactured in the United States of America

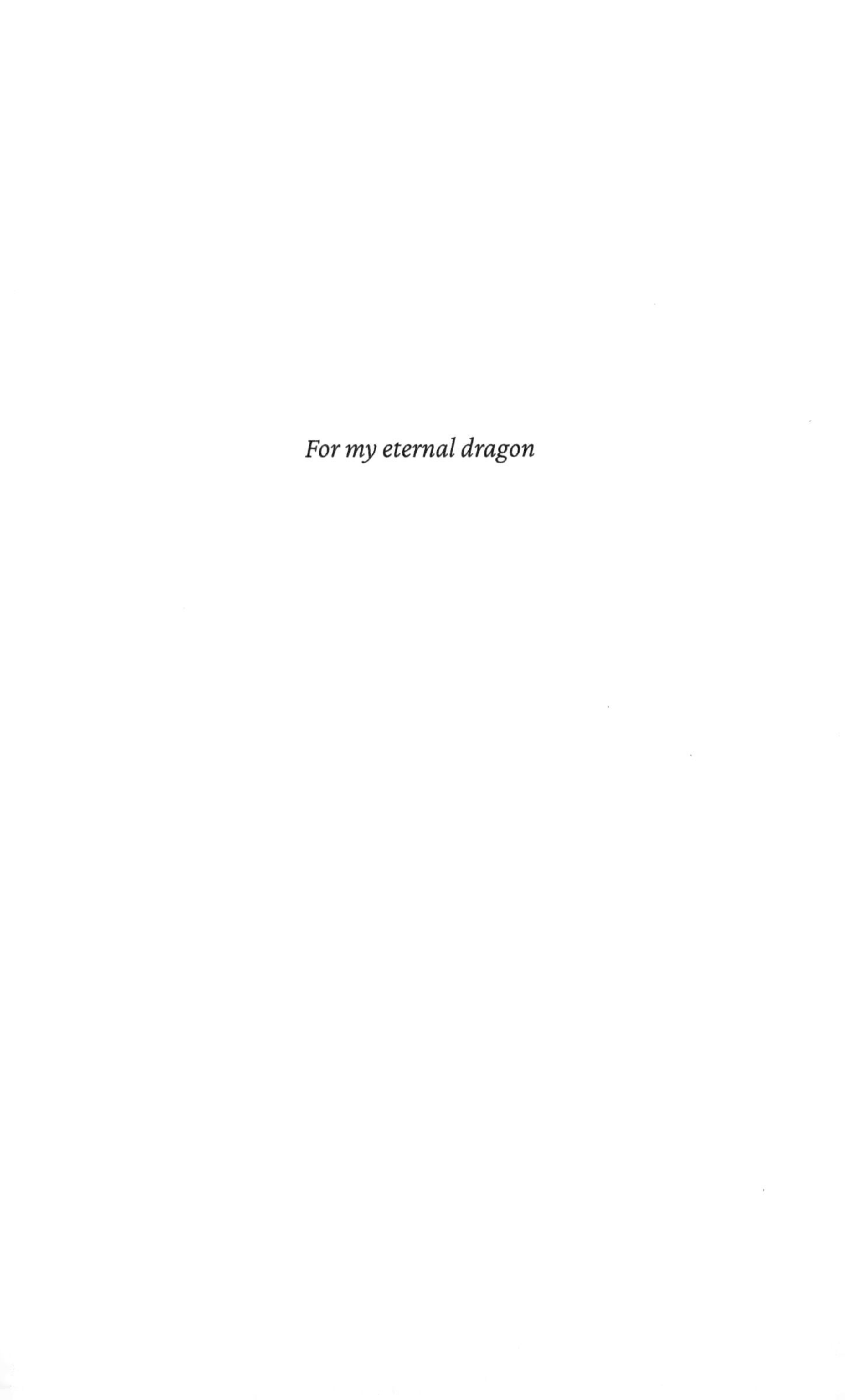

For my eternal dragon

CHAPTER 1
BRAGI

Few things soothed the soul like Mozart filtering through a series of invisible speakers, accompanied by the crackle of a fire, while a storm raged outside. My soul needed a lot of soothing, given the gods I'd betrayed and the tension of hiding from them.

With Vidar gone, I could relax a little, but I knew the remaining members of the TOM board—gods determined to destroy whomever it took to ensure they lived through Ragnarök—wouldn't let me survive for long.

I'd been one of them, and betrayed them. For what? A stunning redhead who was barely more than a quarter of a century old?

If only it were—

The chime of the doorbell, followed by a strong pounding that quickly faded to weak, filled the

1

room.

Once upon a time, I would've had staff to answer that for me. A butler to greet guests and show them to the sitting room, where I could be waiting while they made a grand entrance. But centuries of bathing in the emotions of others had caught up to me. Now my empathy and I preferred to live alone.

Speaking of—the pain radiating from my front step would've suffocated me once upon a time. It was so potent, I couldn't tell who it belonged to. I also couldn't ignore it.

Loneliness, grief, and agony enveloped me as I strode quickly to answer the door. When I opened it, my heart sank. "Magnus?"

She was in her Valkyrie form, but her auburn wings were as tattered as her clothing, and she was using her sword to support her. Slashes and burns cut deep through several parts of her body.

She was supposed to heal immediately. Always. Whoever had done this to her was powerful and knew how to make her injuries last.

She looked up, the clouds in her gaze lifting for a moment as she focused on me. "I didn't know where to go." Her voice barely reached above the rain hammering around her. "Everyone else is... gone."

Magnus stumbled and fell to one knee, and hopelessness spilled from her, sharp and foul when mixed with her other emotions.

I stepped in before she could hit the ground,

scooped her into my arms, and carried her inside and up to my room. No other bed would do tonight; I needed her in the most comfortable room in the house, and where my energy was the strongest.

I set her on my bed and brushed her hair from her battered face. Even unconscious, she radiated fear and the heartbroken ache that came from being betrayed.

"Who did this to you?" I muttered, though she couldn't answer in this condition. Some of her wounds were slowly knitting back together, but not many and not fast enough.

I cut away her clothing. Modesty wasn't a concern with the severity of her injuries. I cleaned and dried her as best I could with her in this condition, dressed the wounds, and wrapped her in fresh clothing and blankets.

Every few minutes, through the entire process, she whimpered or growled or lashed out, but she never woke up. The various pains that radiated from her were cloying.

Cutting myself off from them was an option. When another's emotions were so potent, it took focus, but I could force myself to ignore those feelings.

Being an empath surrounded by gods who fucked and fought all the time had been rough when I was younger. Centuries ago. As I grew older, I learned to revel in the pain and lust and rage others radiated. I absorbed it and fed on it.

A lot of beings—god and human—thought being a god of music and poetry, a bard, was a useless power. But being able to absorb hate and pain, and project it back out, could be as potent as any physical attack.

Tonight I wanted to soothe, rather than harm, the woman lying in my bed. It was tempting to bathe in her fear and rage until it consumed me, but that wouldn't help her. Instead, I summoned a center of calm, to transfer the same to her.

Magnus didn't know it, but she'd saved me. She was loyalty and love and fierceness, all for those she considered family, regardless of the storm she got caught up in. When I first recognized it in her, I resented it. But over time, I learned to crave it.

I may never tell her that, but tonight I could save her in return.

A brush of my fingertips across her forehead, and a push of soothing emotion, and her whimpers and thrashing stopped. Her wounds weren't healing any faster though. If I didn't know any better, if I wasn't looking at her wings and the sword now propped up next to the nightstand, I'd think she was mortal.

The way she used to be. Fragile, but still fierce.

As the night wore on, her wounds seemed to be getting worse instead of better. I couldn't rouse her, and her fever was climbing.

She had friends with healing powers, but they were very much my enemies, and there had to be a reason she was here and not there.

I'd alienated most everyone, regardless of which side of the coming war they stood on.

My options were limited in who I could call to help. I could only think of one individual who could both heal and wouldn't attack either Magnus or me on sight.

I brushed my lips over her forehead—a gesture too intimate for our relationship, but that felt right. "I wouldn't do this for anyone else," I whispered.

CHAPTER 2

NICODEMUS

The phone on my wall rang.

Considering it hadn't gotten calls since manual switchboard operators were replaced with their electric equivalent, it could only mean one thing: some god somewhere had decided to interrupt my morning tea.

I picked up the delicate cup and carried it across the kitchen to the antique device whose bells were jangling loudly.

"Hello," I answered.

"Nicodemus. Good day."

Bragi's familiar voice cut through me, not as sharply as it once had, but enough to kill my interest in my drink. I set my tea aside. "It was. I don't know that it is anymore."

"Join the club. I need you to heal someone."

I pulled the earpiece away to stare at it, then

pressed it back to my ear and spoke into the receiver mounted to the wall. "Beg pardon?"

A lot of immortals could heal, and it seemed for almost as many, it was no big deal. In my case, my tears were the magic ingredient, and they had to be tears of sorrow. Whatever mind of evolution or creation decided that was the way phoenix tears worked could go fuck itself.

"No one else can do this. Even if they could, I don't trust anyone else." Bragi sounded... desperate? That couldn't be right.

I knew better than to be fooled by his lies again. "*Anyone* else can do this. Who did you piss off enough to get hurt?" A better question was—why was I still on the phone?

"It's not for me. Please."

His tone pierced centuries of apathy. If he were in the room, I'd wonder if he was influencing me. Tugging my heartstrings the way he had when we were together. His desperation grabbed me and refused to let go.

"Come get me," I said. I couldn't teleport, though I could fly like the wind when I was in my bird form. Even if I could blink from one place to another, rumor had it Bragi no longer stayed on this plane— he preferred to make his home someplace where he could easily block himself from the whole of the world's emotion.

I grabbed a necklace from the hook on the wall,

where it hung near my keys. I'd wondered on several occasions if I'd ever have a need for the crystal that hung from a leather cord. The talisman that kept me from feeling the influence of gods who were capable of projecting their will.

With Bragi, I'd need it.

He appeared in my kitchen, grabbed my upper arm without a word, and took us back to a bedroom I knew instantly was his, from the decor and the air of emo.

"That's the last time I'm leaving while she's here."

I didn't have to ask who he was talking about. The woman lying on the bed, the auburn-haired Valkyrie who radiated less life than the wooden frame holding up the mattress, captivated me. She was impossible. Another Valkyrie, when there were supposed to be none left. The one I'd dreamed of centuries ago, who didn't exist.

"You found her." I wasn't sure I'd spoken the words aloud.

"No." Bragi's tone was sharp, but his answer meant he knew who I was talking about. "This is Magnus. Not an apparition or a fantasy. She's real."

I approached and knelt next to her, shock spilling through me. "She's got a man's name." It wasn't that I cared, one way or another. But when she'd haunted my dreams, the first time I saw her in my mind, that was part of the vision as well.

"She was raised by them. Us? The Order. Loki gave her the nickname when they adopted her, and it stuck. It has no significance beyond being another way they manipulated her," Bragi said.

I followed the contours of her face with my hand, never making contact, and let what little life energy she had pass over me. She wouldn't be here much longer. Some sort of magic was disassembling her a molecule at a time. Tearing a magic she hadn't been born with from the human she used to be.

That explained why she was a Valkyrie I didn't know.

"Can you fix her?" Bragi radiated ice.

He must be focusing a lot of energy into not giving off any emotion. I almost always felt at least a little from him—he bled feelings the way most people leaked life.

"What happened?" I had my suspicions, based on how she felt, but I needed them confirmed.

"I assume Vidar."

That explained that. She must've really pissed Vidar off. I wanted to be callous and say *no*. To walk away, find a ride home, and pretend Bragi never called.

Seeing the state he was in, and seeing *her*, a creature who shouldn't exist and who was plucked straight from hundreds of years old dreams...

"I can stop the magical damage," I said. "*If* you can make me cry. After that, it's up to her."

Bragi hovered his hand near my face. "*I* can't make you cry. But I can show you what *she's* feeling right now." He cupped my neck and brushed his thumb lightly over my cheek.

The pain that rushed by me was all emotional. Fear. Rage. So much grief it made me gasp. Loss. The kind that no one this young should know. I was drowning in sorrow. A quantity that nearly kept me from bringing her hand to my face to catch the two tears that fell.

I had the presence of mind to fold her arm gently onto the bed, but not much more. When I jerked from Bragi's touch, I gulped the air to make sure I could still breathe.

"Did it work?" His question was laced with concern and fear, but he'd stopped spilling emotion again.

A small thing to be grateful for. I extended my senses again. "My part worked, yes. Now you owe me." A larger debt than he could ever repay. "Start with an explanation."

Bragi filled me in on the last few decades. That the last Valkyrie, the one who died and came back every few decades, was apparently back for good this time.

Good for her. I was all too familiar with the cycle of rebirth, and it was nice to know one of us might be over it.

He told me about how The Order of Mistletoe—

TOM—was crumbling as their leadership either died, went off the deep end like Vidar and Loki were starting to do, or defected, like Bragi had. How the potential gods that prophecy had predicted were showing up everywhere; a whole new generation of immortals. And that somewhere along the way, he'd had a change of heart and decided perhaps burning the world to the ground was a bad idea.

I suspected that it had something to do with the woman in his bed. "That's all well and good, but I meant tell me about her." I needed to know who had broken him to the point where he sacrificed pride to call me.

"You already know she was one of their soldiers. She got out as things were crumbling. She's close enough to Kirby that when Kirby gained the power to make more Valkyries, Magnus was the first. Now she's immortal."

Great. I could've figured most of those details out on my own. "How did she end up like this, and why are you the one helping her?" There was no earthly way I could ignore how much like my dreams she was. I knew that face—it had haunted me for decades after I first saw it in my mind.

"We brought them onto the TOM campus as kids," Bragi said. "Twelve or thirteen, all of them without existing families, and all of them with the potential to become an immortal. Vidar sought them out, Loki recruited them, and Hel trained them as killers."

I'd had a vague idea of what TOM was doing, but only from the perspective of *hunting future gods*. I'd been fine with ignoring the workings of the system, just as I was fine with locking myself away from most of humanity for the last hundred or so years.

The kids in the town I lived near taught me enough that I knew what computers were, and that they fit in the palm of the hand rather than taking up an entire room, but I preferred to read about all of that rather than live it.

Now I found myself in the awkward position of needing to learn more about the world of gods that I'd ignored for so long. "What was your part in it all?"

Bragi turned his gaze to Magnus.

Silence settled between us.

And there was my answer. "You fucking asshole."

"I stopped because of her."

"Oh, yes. I can see how that's atonement." I swallowed the bile rising in my throat. The reason he and I had ended our relationship, the reason I refused to speak to him, was because he'd used his ability to project emotion to influence me when we were together. He insisted he'd only done it once, but how could I trust him, knowing it had always been an option?

He had emotionally pushed those soldiers, those children, to comply. To feel whatever his counterparts needed them to at that school.

I was going to be ill. However, I refused to let him see my response or feel it, so I tucked the reaction under layers of disdain.

Bragi raked his fingers through his hair. "Several of the recruits—"

"Children." I couldn't let him gloss over that point.

"Several of the children Vidar brought in turned out to be his." Regret washed through the room.

Someone was bleeding feelings.

With a shake of his head, Bragi's emotions vanished from the air. "One of them connected with Magnus almost immediately. The two of them are closer than sisters. I don't know the whole story, Magnus wasn't in any condition to tell me when she showed up, but I know the two of them were actively hunting Vidar."

There was more to this story, for instance, what about this woman had stopped Bragi's destructive path, but I wasn't sure I wanted to drag it out of him.

I was willing to stay here and make sure this Valkyrie, Magnus, survived, so I already understood at least on some level that she was compelling.

My reasons were different, though. I was staring at the tortured face of a woman who had haunted my dreams centuries before she was born, and I needed to know why.

So many whys.

CHAPTER 3

MAGNUS

At the sound of a gunshot, my heart sank. It shouldn't. This was a room full of immortals, and bullets shouldn't mean a fucking thing. But foreboding swallowed me and nausea surged in my gut, while a tiny little voice in my mind whispered that if I did things differently this time, I could save them.

This time?

Save who?

I stood in an office that reeked of Vidar, across from him, with Fen and Dahlia by my side. Except Fen was on his knees, tendrils of death spreading up his neck and down his arm.

Why didn't I stop that?

I couldn't have. Could I?

I had already extended the shield that was one of

my powers as a Valkyrie, but that was too little, too late.

The panic that raced through me was tempered by a strange sense of Deja vu, and at the same time, the feeling of being removed from it all. Like I wasn't part of this.

I screamed at Dahlia to get us out of here. She'd brought us in, her powers as a dragon allowed her to teleport where neither Fen nor I could. Her powers should allow a lot more than that, but she was frozen.

"*To me.*" Bragi shouldn't be here. We didn't trust him to fight by our sides, especially against Vidar. But he stood at the edge of my shield, reaching for us.

He was safe. The others didn't believe that, but it was true, my gut said so. Of course, my gut had been wrong about Vidar, but this was different. I *knew* it.

Dahlia grabbed Fen's hand, and I grabbed hers and dropped the shield to take Bragi's. In a blink we were back in NEON.

Fighting Vidar—correction, Vidar kicking our asses—was chaos, but this was a clusterfuck. Everything blurred together as I tried to call the only god we'd seen cure what was happening to Fen.

Magic bullets. The kind meant to kill immortals who refused to embrace their tie to death.

Given how willing the gods were to kill, I

wouldn't think that would be a very effective weapon, but apparently it was.

Fen lay in bed, writhing in agony as death gnawed a path through his system. I left message after message, trying to reach Min or someone who could.

Frey, who had been Fen's lover and mate for centuries, had Bragi pressed to the wall and was threatening him. Torturing him. Not with a physical onslaught, but with a wave of the potent emotions Frey felt having to watch Fen suffer this way.

This wasn't right. Bragi had saved us, and he wasn't to blame for what was happening now. It would hurt Dahlia to see me do this, she loved Fen and Frey so much, but I wasn't acting against Frey, I was acting in favor of Bragi. I'd beg her forgiveness when this was over and Fen was healed.

I asked Frey to stop. To make him see reason and not hurt Bragi.

The way Dahlia looked at me sliced me to my core.

This entire thing felt choppy. As if things were happening too fast or too slowly. Nothing moved at the right speed.

Bragi vanished.

Fucker. I'd stuck up for him. He could've stayed and made the others see he wasn't the bad guy.

I hated seeing Dahlia like this. Worrying about Fen.

I needed to make this right. How? Not a clue, but it started with confronting Vidar the smart way. Just me. One of my strengths, not the magical kind, the type I'd actually been born with, was watching people and learning. I knew a lot more about Vidar than he realized.

Like how to find him again. Even though we'd just left the TOM compound he was in, it was unlikely he'd stay at that base. He was a being of habit and patterns though, like most creatures.

The portal that would take me to him was easy to activate. While I'd left my friends behind, fighting with the fallout of confronting him, he was conducting business like it was any other day.

Fucking asshole.

I didn't give him a chance to speak. Lies and taunting would spill from his mouth and I was going to slaughter him regardless of what he said.

And then the entire setting changed. We weren't in an office, it looked more like a concrete cavern. Vidar was nowhere to be seen, but the attacks came from everywhere all at once. I lost track of anything but trying to find him, and keeping myself from getting hit. With every strike from a ball of flame or a crack of lightning, I felt it through my entire body.

The onslaught poured in so fast, I didn't have time to heal. It came from inside my shield. It tore me down.

I wouldn't let things end this way.

When Dahlia and Fen appeared in the room, Fen healed and full of rage, I'd never been so relieved. They joined the fight without hesitation. The three of us worked well together—a well-oiled team. Dahlia and I had always had the rhythm when we did anything.

It didn't matter.

Vidar hit us again and again. From every angle. Slicing down Fen and Dahlia. Shredding them to pieces until Dahlia was on her knees and Fen was panting.

They were both down. Not moving. I needed to check on them, but I needed to keep Vidar at bay. I could heal most things, even if I was struggling, maybe I could help them.

If I pulled the shield tightly enough, Vidar shouldn't be able to hit us. It would give me time to tend to my friends.

I swooped toward them at high speed.

A wall of flame erupted between us, and I flew through it. The heat tore at my flesh, doing more damage than it should, but I needed to get to Dahlia.

When I came out the other side, I pulled up short. It was too late. Her body vanished in an explosion of ash and flame.

She was gone.

But she couldn't be.

But she was.

Fury and grief consumed me with as much

agony as the fire raging around me, and I flew at Vidar, sword drawn. I made contact, a direct hit, and didn't let up. I sliced and tore, summoning everything I could find inside me. My Valkyrie was pushed to depths I didn't realize I was capable of, until Vidar was gone too. Dead. Obliterated.

My legs didn't work right. Walking took a force of will I wasn't sure I had. Dahlia was gone. My best friend. My sister. The one person in this world who had my back.

And I didn't have enough strength to cry for her.

I need to go back to Frey. To tell him what happened. But if he destroyed me in his grief, the way he'd threatened to do to Bragi, I wouldn't be able to seek vengeance for Dahlia's death.

If I had a little time, then I could hunt down anyone else involved in this. When that was done, Frey could have at me.

Where was safe? Nowhere.

Bragi.

Long enough to heal. A few hours maybe. Magical Valkyrie recovering powers and all that.

The pit in my heart would live there for eternity though. That spot Dahlia held. She couldn't be gone, but she was. I'd see it with my own eyes.

I missed her so much already that the grief ached more than my wounds. I'd let her die. She came after me, to help, and she was gone because of it.

Bragi opened his door.

I didn't even remember making the trip. How did I get here?

"Magnus?" He radiated concern.

"I didn't know where else to go." I barely heard my own voice. "Everyone else is… gone."

At the sound of a gunshot, my heart sank.

I could save them.

Save who?

I had extended the shield that was one of my powers as a Valkyrie, but that was too little, too late.

The panic that raced through me was tempered by a strange sense of Deja vu, and at the same time, the feeling of being removed from it all. Like I wasn't part of this.

I screamed at Dahlia to get us out of here. She'd brought us in, her powers as a dragon allowed her to teleport where neither Fen nor I could. Her powers should allow a lot more than that, but she was frozen.

"*To me.*" Bragi shouldn't be here. We didn't trust him to fight by our sides, especially against Vidar. But he stood at the edge of my shield, reaching for us.

"*Magnus.*" His tone grew insistent, but his lips weren't moving. "*Magnus. I need you to come back to me.*"

I didn't… He was right there. I reached for him, but my hand slipped through his. "I'm trying." My voice didn't work. I tried to force the words out, but the harder I pushed, the less voice and air I had.

"Magnus. Please."

I'd never heard Bragi beg before. I'd rarely heard any god beg, and I knew more than the standard number of gods who had been in desperate situations.

"I'm trying." On the —*ing* my voice caught. I felt the sound. Heard it.

I grasped the sensation and reached for both words and Bragi. As my hand met his, a shout tore from my throat.

I sat straight up with a scream. This wasn't Vidar's office or Frey's. I wasn't in NEON. What was going on?

"*Thank you.*" The muttered sound of relief came from next to me.

Bragi. He was kneeling next to me, my hand clutched in both of his, and his forehead pressed to my knuckles.

I was in a bed I didn't recognize, and a man I didn't recognize watched us from a few feet away. He was pretty. Fiery red hair. Penetrating brown eyes. He bled life—I saw it rolling off him in flames.

"Where am I?" My brain was still caught in the nightmare, and I struggled to shake off the potent visions. The fear and grief.

Bragi let go of my hand and stepped back. "My house. How much do you remember?"

"I don't..." As if my thoughts were knocked loose by his question, reality crashed in around me in an avalanche of grief.

That wasn't a nightmare, it was reality.

Dahlia was gone. Fenrir.

I'd seen them die. I hadn't been able to stop it from happening.

Sobs wracked my body, shaking me so hard it hurt. I didn't know the last time I'd cried, but I couldn't stop, even if the grief tore me apart.

"They're all gone. All of them. Gone." I muttered the words over and over, not wanting to believe them, but not having any choice.

CHAPTER 4

BRAGI

There were a few key points in my life where I'd been conflicted to the point where it almost immobilized me. Was it a coincidence that the man sitting in a chair near my bed was part of more than one of those, and the woman in my arms was as well?

I held Magnus as her grief threatened to tear her apart. I felt every sob and cough and gasp, both in my body and heart, and I couldn't make myself let her go or turn off my own reaction to her emotions.

The first time I met her, when she was a student, she was already seventeen. I met most of the soldiers at TOM far earlier in their lives, because I was the carrot and Vidar was the stick. A visit from me was meant to provide an emotional push for those students who were out of line.

Magnus was sarcastic, and she talked back, but

she wasn't the same kind of defiant. She was also loyal. Loving. Hiding how much she cared behind a wall meant to protect her classmates as much as herself.

As I held her now, letting her weep through her loss, that wall was gone. A piece of her was broken, and she just kept repeating, "She's gone. Dahlia's dead."

I wanted to push back more than the assurance I was here for her, but I wouldn't. I refused to send any false emotion into her, even to temporarily make her feel better. Not just because Nico—Nico—watched me.

The first day I met her, I'd been drawn to who she was at her core, and the first time she smiled at me, it didn't matter that I was one of those bullshit TOM smiles meant to charm and disarm. I felt the genuine emotion underneath, and refused to corrupt that.

It was the same now, regardless of how much it hurt to feel what she did, and regardless of how wrong it was to enjoy holding her.

As her crying slowed, Nico and I coaxed the story out of her. How she'd gone after Vidar on her own, because he'd hurt Fen and Dahlia. Because he was an asshole who deserved to be put down.

I couldn't argue her reasons, but I felt an intense guilt. Minutes before she made that decision, I'd been there. If I'd stuck around, could I have stopped her? Gone with her? Could I have prevented any of this?

When Fen and Dahlia followed her, Vidar had beaten them all. Magnus's story was sparse on details beyond *he killed her. Them. He slaughtered them,* but something about it wasn't right.

Vidar had tricks up his sleeve. Magic he rarely accessed and more skills than he should have, thanks to the way he'd bastardized fae and dragon magic, but for him to stomp Fenrir so completely...

But Magnus had witnessed the entire thing. There was no doubt or deception in her story. She was a pillar of grief.

Magnus shot to her feet, her eyes wide, startling me. "I need to tell Frey." Panic spilled from her. Regret. Guilt. "I need to tell him Fen is gone and beg his forgiveness and—"

"And what?" I grabbed her wrist. "Are you going to throw yourself on his proverbial sword? Sacrifice yourself for their loss?" Odds were low that he'd treat her the way he had me, when he blamed me for Fen's injuries, but odds weren't non-existent. I was keeping her here until she was at least well enough to put away her Valkyrie wings.

She scrubbed her face with her free hand, fidgeting in tiny circles where she stood on my carpet. "He needs to know. He needs to hear it from someone who cares."

"I'll tell him." From a distance. Via phone.

"No, no, no, no, no." She shook her head vigorously, until I stepped in, cupped her cheeks between my palms, and stopped her.

I cracked a little at the sight of her stress, and used the contact to let a whisper of a suggestion slip through. Not a lot. A hint of calm. To keep her from worrying herself to death and to prevent her from going to Frey.

"Sit. Rest," I whispered. "I'll make you something to eat. Nico will keep you company."

His raised eyebrow didn't hide his accusing look. He knew what I'd done. "I'd be happy to sit with you." He meant it. "I'm Nicodemus. Nico for short. Pleasure to meet you, though I'm sorry it's under these circumstances."

"Same." Magnus's voice was uncharacteristically meek. She sank back onto the edge of the bed, her wings wrapped around her like a tattered blanket, and he settled into the spot next to her.

I was fully aware of what Nico saw when he looked at her, and my taking advantage of that was a manipulation I didn't feel bad about. She wasn't healing, and I could see why not, but I couldn't tell what was causing it. The encounter with Vidar had severed her from her magic, either psychologically or physically. If it was the latter, Nico's healing may be needed again, and if it was the former, she'd need all the support and distraction possible.

In the kitchen, I assembled ingredients, and set

to work making waffles with fruit and cream. The soldiers were raised on a steady diet of all the things a growing body under intense physical duress needed. They got their greens, their protein, appropriate doses of everything.

It had all been regulated, and it left a large number of them with a sweet tooth. For a TOM soldier, sex was part of the job, but chocolate and whipped cream were indulgences. A treat few of them associated with school or training.

While I was waiting for the waffle maker, my phone rang. I glanced at the screen, then did a double take. That was Vidar's number, but according to Magnus, he should be dead.

I should've known better. Was this him calling to chide me for my betrayal? For playing both sides, in favor of keeping Magnus safe. I'd had to reveal my deception to save her, not even forty-eight hours ago. "Hello," I answered coolly.

"Bragi the Betrayer." Vidar didn't sound like a dead man. "It's certainly got a ring to it."

"So does Vidar the Silent God, but it's never held true." I summoned the nickname given to him in myths and retellings. Several of which he'd been responsible for propagating.

His chuckle was dry and humorless. A bit like him. "Are you caring for a specific Valkyrie as we speak?"

My blood ran cold. My home and its inhabitants

should be undetectable here, thanks to a combination of my magic and the corner of the fae realm I resided in. I was going to call his bluff and assume he didn't actually know. "I'm talking to you. I'm making coffee. I'm not caring for anyone."

"Hmm. Well, if she comes knocking, keep her away from Dahlia."

I couldn't reveal too much, or I'd give away how I knew. "It's my understanding Dahlia is dead. Then again, you're supposed to be as well." Would I have heard that from anyone besides Magnus? I still had other contacts in TOM. How many of his soldiers thought he was gone?

"In that case, continue to believe that."

I had so many questions, and didn't trust that he'd give me any usable answers. "You know I betrayed you. What makes you think—"

"Because I know why you did it, and that she's with you now. Keep her there long enough for me to destroy Fenrir, and I'll consider us even."

I doubted that. I also didn't want to see Fenrir actually die—it was a relief to know that he and Dahlia were alive. However, while their safety was nice, it wasn't an intense, driving motivator in my life. I had Magnus in my grasp. I could hold onto her...

Was that fucked-up and wrong? Of course. Knowing as much didn't stop me from entertaining the possibility.

"Keep your prize," Vidar said. "Or I can finish what I started with Magnus, as well. I'm doing you a favor."

Uh-huh. "I doubt that."

"I don't want to watch the world burn any more than you do."

I heard that a lot. I'd said it a few times myself. There were a surprisingly large number of ways to interpret a statement like his. "No," I said. "You just want to lightly scorch it and remake it in your image."

"It won't impact you unless you get in the way. Why do you give a fuck? Besides, you have *her* now."

I hung up and tossed the phone aside, not caring that it clattered loudly on the table and slid to a stop at the edge.

Magnus's grief was barely muted, despite her being in the other room. A few words, and I could change that.

And if I did, she'd go after Vidar again. She may not come back this time.

The world would be a bleak place without Magnus in it. I loathed the thought enough that it made my gut churn.

I didn't have to keep this secret forever, or even as long as Vidar had asked me to. Once Magnus was better, once she'd recovered, she could know the truth. She'd hate me when she found out. The kind of loathing I could dine on for centuries.

But I'd have her until then, and she'd be alive when all was said and done.

I finished preparing the food, wiped any trace of my reaction to the conversation with Vidar from my face or mind, and returned to Magnus and Nico in the bedroom.

Whether or not to comply with Vidar's request was an easy decision, and the answer was the one that kept Magnus safe and close to me.

CHAPTER 5
NICODEMUS

I didn't need Bragi's empathy to feel Magnus's sorrow.

Her legs hung over the side of the bed and she watched as they kicked back and forth, toes dragging along the carpet. She gripped the edge of the mattress hard enough I saw the strain in her knuckles. There didn't seem to be an appropriate means of breaking the silence, so I didn't try.

"Why are you here?" Magnus asked.

I didn't have an answer to that question. I still wasn't completely sure why I'd agreed to come, or why I hadn't left. "Bragi asked me to heal you."

"Are the two of you that close?" Her tone was raw, but the tears were gone. "He asks a favor and you say *yes*?"

"No."

Her *hmm* was so soft I barely heard it. "No

offense, but I don't feel completely healed." Magnus held her arm straight out and rolled it back and forth as she flexed her fingers.

"You're not. But that's not my doing." I wanted to believe this was better than comforting a grieving soul, but it felt cold. Removed.

"It's because I'm broken, isn't it?" Her voice cracked on the last words. She drew in a long breath through her nostrils, and exhaled slowly through her mouth. It wasn't accurate to say she was encased in a shell or wearing a mask, but she was tucking a lot away.

I'd question that opinion, I might even wonder if she was fine, if I hadn't had a taste of the emotion brewing inside her while she slept. How was I supposed to answer her question?

"They taught us in school that sometimes silence is the loudest answer of all." Magnus scooted away, into the middle of the bed and crossed her legs.

They taught us in school... So she truly was one of Hel's soldier babies. "Something is keeping you from healing, yes," I said. "You shouldn't have needed me in the first place."

"Breakfast." Bragi's interruption was both welcome and horrible timing.

I wanted to keep probing for answers, but I suspected if I did, she would probe in return.

Magnus fiddled with a loose thread on the blanket beneath her, rather than meet Bragi's gaze.

"Thank you." Her words were clipped and emotionless.

Bragi set the tray in front of her. "You need to eat. It will help you recover."

"Okay." Magnus's nod was her only real movement.

"Nico, may I speak with you for a moment," Bragi said.

Magnus looked up. "If you're keeping secrets, I will find out."

She was intriguing.

"I don't doubt it." Bragi looked at me while he replied to her. He nodded at the door. "I'm going to ask my other guest if he's staying or not, because we're about to hide."

"I don't hide from anything." The edge that sliced into Magnus's voice was abrupt and sharp.

"*Hide* was the wrong word." Bragi's response came without hesitation. "We're making a tactical retreat to regroup."

Magnus twisted her mouth. "You can phrase it however you'd like. It's still hiding. Vidar may be the one who ki—did this—but the entire TOM board had a hand in the events that led us here, and you know who they are."

"And *you* need to heal to the point where you can do something with that information," Bragi said.

With a tilt of her head, she studied him. "When

the time comes, you won't stand in my way." She didn't phrase it as a question.

"I'll tell you every name and location I have. No games. No bullshit. When the time comes. Nico, I'd still like to speak with you."

Fascinating dynamic. "All right." I followed Bragi into the hallway.

He left the bedroom door open, giving him a direct line of sight to Magnus. "She can't hear us." But he could still watch her.

I was both bothered, and jealous I couldn't easily maneuver myself into a similar angle. Why was she so compelling? How did she exist? "The answer is *no*. I'm not staying. I can't do anymore for her, and the crying is fucking taxing." I was lying. As soon as I refused, I heard my own bullshit. It was true, the tears hurt, so why did I want Bragi to change my mind?

"I have to hide her, me, this place completely, until she's better," Bragi said. "That means no coming or going. If she needs you again..."

This was ridiculous. The answer was easy. "No."

"You can't lie to me the way you can to yourself."

I glared at Bragi. "Stay the fuck out of my heart, and stop projecting your own feelings on me."

"You'd *know* if I was projecting. Do you really want to play this game of *let's pretend* with me?"

"I don't want to play *any* games with you. That's why I left." That and I'd found out he used his empathy to manipulate my emotions. He'd sworn he only did it once, but that was simply the one time I caught him. It had only taken him a moment to do the same to Magnus today. To give her an emotional nudge to calm her down.

Proof that nothing had changed.

Which meant I couldn't leave her here alone with him, either.

Fuck.

"I'll stay." It wasn't as though I was doing something important with my time at home.

"Thank you." Bragi sounded sincere.

Unlike him, I didn't have the ability to read the lies wafting from him in waves, however, I did have the experience to tell me he was hiding *something*.

When we stepped into the bedroom again, Magnus looked up, and I swore she wore a blank, glazed over expression. The look vanished behind muted sorrow before I could be certain.

"You haven't eaten," I said. "You need to."

"Okay." She didn't move.

I could tell myself again and again not to be drawn to her because of a dream I had hundreds of years ago. A vision that became a short-term obsession, that I had described to Bragi in such detail that he helped me search for a woman who didn't exist. Or I could admit that was at least part of what was keeping me here by Magnus's side, so I could move past the fascination.

Like a normal person.

Sure.

I sat next to her on the bed again, plucked out a strawberry from the dish Bragi brought, dipped it in whipped cream, and pressed it to her lips.

The way she bit into the fruit was mechanical rather than erotic. She chewed and swallowed as if on autopilot.

Feeding her the waffles, a forkful at a time, wasn't the sweet, dream-like fantasy one might expect. It was heartrending to see her operating on auto-pilot. Responding because part of her was programmed to comply, rather than because she cared.

She ate about half the food, then scooted away. "I'd like to sleep."

"All right." Based on her story and her pain, she'd lost her sister and best friend. Acting *off* was the most normal thing about this situation. I pulled the tray away and handed it to Bragi.

Magnus lay down and curled into a fetal position.

I covered her with the blanket, and beat back the impulse to kiss her on the forehead to help soothe her. It would be nice to offer a verbal reassurance or any form of comfort, but nothing was appropriate for the situation. "I'll be here if you need anything."

"Okay." She closed her eyes.

Bragi and I left Magnus to sleep. When we stepped into the hallway, he opened his mouth.

I held up my index finger. "No. I'm here for her. I want to hear as little as possible from you, and don't you dare touch me. No accidental brushes against me or *oopsies*."

Bragi pursed his lips and his nostrils flared. "That's fair."

The next few days—week?—passed in a blur. Time moved differently in this realm, and being cut off from the outside world combined with the fact that Bragi didn't keep any clocks on display, made it difficult to gauge how long it had been.

Magnus tossed and turned in her sleep, and woke up either in tears or rage. Bragi and I took turns keeping an eye on her and making sure she ate when she was conscious enough to do so. Mostly though, she slept.

Magnus was healing, but it was the way a human would. The abrasions on her arms and face scabbed over rather than vanishing. Her wings remained exposed, though she kept them tucked close to her back most of the time, and the feathers were singed at the tips.

Some sort of anomaly was keeping her from getting better. If I tried to search her aura, the light swam around her, making her look like a reflection in a cracked mirror.

When I wasn't watching her, I spent my time in

the library. Bragi's was impressive. It had always been my favorite room in his house. Walls filled with bookshelves, and more shelves in the middle of the room. He had tomes from across the centuries—a combination of history and lore. Several of the volumes were his recounting of both, and others were from the various people who thought they could call him a contemporary, over the centuries.

He was a skilled story-teller and always had been.

Then again, that was the problem. The stories didn't stop, even in everyday life. However, I had enough wisdom and appreciation for a good tale that I could lose myself in the older tomes regardless.

"Excuse me." The quiet words cut through my focus, and a fist squeezed around my heart before I registered who the voice belonged to.

I looked up to see Magnus standing in the doorway to the library, watching me with a clearer expression than she'd worn since I arrived. Her hair hung in wet ringlets around her shoulders, and her face and arms shone pale pink from being freshly scrubbed. She wasn't healed, not by a longshot, but death no longer lingered in her aura.

Given she was a Valkyrie, that was slightly problematic, but it was bounds better than before.

"Hello." Oh, I was brilliant. Perhaps I could

borrow some of Bragi's gift for words long enough to have a conversation?

She let out a tiny huff that might have been a laugh or a sigh, but at least it was a real reaction. "Did you save me?"

"Yes."

She stepped into the room, moving with the grace of someone trained to be aware of their every step. "I know you've been here almost since I arrived, but I don't feel like I know anything about you beyond your name."

"Would you like to?" I asked.

"Yes."

CHAPTER 6
MAGNUS

I remembered everything that happened.

All of it.

It was as if the fight—losing Dahlia—was etched into my mind in exquisitely torturous detail. Trauma, injury, and several days of fever hadn't dulled any of the vivid images.

I also remembered what came after, though that wasn't as clear. Bragi sitting with me. The new man, Nico.

Though, neither of them was here now.

It wasn't odd for me to wake up in a stranger's bed, but knowing whose it was did feel strange. I felt better than I had since I arrived. My thoughts were clearer and my joints didn't ache as much.

They shouldn't ache at all, and that was worrisome.

I climbed from the bed, and stumbled when my

feet first hit the floor. Was this normal human weakness, or more? My wings were still here, I couldn't get them to vanish, but I felt disconnected from most of my Valkyrie powers.

Was this what it felt like for Dahlia when she couldn't access her dragon?

The question carried an onslaught of fresh pain. A reminder of her, of what had been taken from me. From her. My body screamed for me to curl up in a ball and mourn her forever.

Anger surged in.

Fuck that. I wasn't going to whimper and shirk. Dahlia deserved more. When we left TOM, we swore we were done letting them tell us how to think and feel, and Vidar did not get the last word in my emotions. His dying did not give him permission to push feeling on me.

If I was the kind of person who gave up when things got hard, I wouldn't have survived this long. I wanted vengeance in Dahlia's name, and I was going to have it.

There was a folded pile of clothes sitting on a chair by the bed. Closer examination revealed that the leggings, strategically ripped jeans, and *Hello Kitty* racerback tank top were my size and looked a lot like something I would pick out for myself. But I hadn't.

Forcing myself to move, despite the ache in my heart, took all my strength, which meant I didn't have enough left to think about why Bragi had such a perfectly *me* outfit waiting for me.

One foot in front of the other. The only way to sate my anger was to keep moving. To not let the grief drag me down. I moved into the bathroom. The freestanding claw tub was inviting. I could soak in there for hours.

But I didn't want to think about what that would do to my wings. I settled for washing my hair separately, and showering, taking great care to keep as much water as I could from my feathers, which were damaged to the point they wouldn't repel water. When I was done, I felt refreshed, but not better.

Would I ever feel better?

Destroying every fucking member of the TOM board who wasn't Bragi sounded like a good start.

I dressed, struggling for a moment to work the top around my wings, and ran a comb through my hair. There was no make-up in here. It was an odd sensation to be relieved that at least Bragi didn't know enough about me to buy me eyeliner and lipstick.

Where was he, anyway? Where was Nico?

I wandered from the bedroom and strolled down the hallway to the first set of open doors. When I stepped into the doorway, my breath caught in my throat.

What a glorious library. Dahlia and I could spend hours in a place like this.

There was that pain again. So sharp it was like a knife in my heart.

Nico sat at the edge of the shelves, on a flowery, upholstered loveseat, engrossed in whatever he was reading. He didn't have the same ethereal look now that my fever had broken, but he was still pretty. I hated to interrupt, but I also needed company.

"Excuse me." I kept my voice quiet, hoping not to startle him too badly.

He jerked his head up, eyes wide, and stared at me for a moment. "Hello."

A light sigh escaped my chest. This was so normal amid everything else. If I let go just a touch, would instinct and training kick in and take over this conversation or would I collapse into grief? "Did you save me?" I was pretty sure Bragi didn't have any healing magic, and apparently mine wasn't working right.

"Yes," Nico said.

"I know you've been here almost since I arrived, but I don't feel like I know anything about you beyond your name."

"Would you like to?" he asked.

Anything that took my mind off my own issues for at least a few seconds. "Yes."

He set his book aside and patted the empty seat next to him, and I padded across an intricate rug to settle next to him. I tucked one sock-covered foot under the other leg. "How?" If I let the words flow without much thought, I could do this. "How did you save me?"

"I cried." His response came so easily, so quickly, it was as if he wasn't guarding his words at all. "I'm a phoenix." He'd even offered information I hadn't asked for.

"I didn't know phoenixes were real."

He chuckled. "That always amuses me."

"That people don't believe in you?" I could let the questions flow, as long as it was more about him than me. Like a casual interrogation, but without the malice behind it.

"Essentially, yes. You've met gods. You're a Valkyrie because a woman who's had more than a dozen lives shared her power with you."

"Just because gods are real doesn't mean the force is." I understood his logic, but it was flawed. "There's still a line that divides reality and fiction."

His smile wasn't too bright, but it was soothing. "That's a reasonable point."

"Does that mean when you die, you come back to life?" As soon as the question passed my lips, I wanted to take it back. Not because it was a bad question, but because *unlike Dahlia* lodged in my throat and threatened to choke me.

Nico placed a finger under my chin and raised my gaze to his. Looking him in the eye was harder than I expected, but I refused to turn away. "Yes," he said.

I needed a new topic, but without the conversation stuttering. "Neat trick. I wonder what other kinds of beings are out there that I don't know about."

"Leprechauns. I don't know if you've ever met one of those. Fickle beings." He furrowed his brow. "Unicorns."

"I did know about the unicorns." I'd heard stories from Kirby—the Valkyrie Nico had been talking about—and Gwydion, one of her mates. Dirty, kinky stories. So much for maidens and innocence.

He dropped his hand, but I didn't drop my chin. I liked the green of his eyes tinged with gold flecks.

"There are kind, caring gods," he said.

I almost laughed, but that would be wrong. "I've met one or two." Again, two of Kirby's mates. Frey. Fen. And now I was thinking of Dahlia again. She'd like Nico already. Though he was guarded, it wasn't so much that it felt like he was trying to deceive. She'd never learned how to not be a nervous talker. I loved that about her.

Goddess, I missed her. I couldn't believe she was gone. I was gasping for air through the grief as the room spun around me.

A hand on mine gave me a place to focus that wasn't my grief.

"A word of advice, from someone with experience, if I may?" Nico said

I didn't deal well with unsolicited advice on the best of days. I doubted I'd appreciate it now. "I swear to all that's holy, if you tell me dealing with death gets easier the longer I live..."

"No. *Creation*, no. Why would I say something so cruel? I was going to say that it always hurts."

"Thanks. That's so much better." I let my sarcasm leak out.

He twisted his mouth. "The ache means what you're feeling is real. The love. The hurt. Don't fight it, but don't lose yourself in it either."

"I want to avenge it." That was more than I meant to admit aloud. Maybe the jumbled words wouldn't make sense to him.

Warmth shone in his gaze every time he glanced at me. The kind of understanding that wrapped around me in a way I didn't deserve. "I'd never stand in your way if that was what you wanted. Until you can have that, I'm offering you sympathy and understanding," Nico said. "When your sadness is so dense you can't breathe through it. When the rage is so potent it devours your soul. When the sun peeks through long enough for you to catch a glimpse, and the guilt kicks in because of it. I understand. You're allowed to feel what you feel."

I'd never been told that before. Not in those words. My entire teenage life, I'd been taught that my feelings were the worst thing I could give a voice to, and I was tempted to tell him I was *not* allowed that. This hurt so fucking much, I couldn't ignore it.

"I can't go after anyone in this condition." I'd been at my best when I faced off against Vidar, and now didn't even have control over my wings. As much as I wanted to go *now*, and hunt down anyone associated with what Vidar had done, as much as I wanted to call Frey, beg his forgiveness, and gather him and every one of our friends to launch a full-force attack...

I couldn't. Not in my condition.

Nothing in my life had been so maddening as my current inability to act.

CHAPTER 7

BRAGI

Given how hard Magnus's dreams were on me, they had to be a hundred times worse for her. I didn't pity myself, but I did need to take the occasional breather so I could be available when she needed me. It was vital I cut myself off from most of her feelings, only leaving enough of a connection to sense a shift.

I didn't realize I'd dozed until I woke up to the emotion in the air feeling different. More erratic—which was saying a lot. There was a hint of contentment mixed in with her sorrow and fury. And attraction?

The thread was easy to follow to the library, where I found her sitting next to Nico. My jealousy surged, but I kept the feeling contained to me.

When Magnus saw me, her attraction split, making my own feelings more like a sour-sweet candy. There was trust, too. I hated that she trusted me, but I wasn't going to be the one to tell her she was wrong. Because under all the new feelings she radiated, Magnus remained at the core. Her loyalty. The pureness in her heart, despite the potent need for vengeance. Most people would argue that both weren't possible at the same time.

I was getting drunk on the blend, so most people were wrong.

"Am I interrupting?" I didn't actually give a fuck. I was inserting myself in the conversation.

"No." Magnus's answer overlapped with Nico's, "Yes."

She scooted closer to him and, despite the furniture only being made for one or two people, patted the now empty spot. "Join us?"

Nico's look and feelings were the loudest *don't you dare* I'd never heard.

I took a seat next to Magnus. *How are you feeling* was always a dangerous question for me to ask, because emotions surged when people heard it. Hers were already cranked to a high volume. I settled for, "I'm glad to see you up and about."

"Thank you." She deflated a bit. Survivor's guilt. "For everything. For taking me in and calling Nico and for saving me."

Saving hardly felt like the right word. Still, "don't mention it. I'd do it all again in a heartbeat. How's your recovery going?"

"I don't think it is." She pushed to her feet and paced in front of us, her frustration surging. "I feel so…"

Tired. Guilty. Furious. Turned on. More guilt. Stuck. Lonely. Sad.

"Mortal," she said.

"Ah. That I can help with."

She stared at me with disbelief. "You can help me be not mortal?"

Perhaps I should have held that card close to my chest a little longer. "Yes."

"How? Like, how does it work? Why haven't you done it yet? Let's do it now. Why didn't you ever do this for us at TOM? Could you have done the same for…" Magnus trailed off with a sigh, her grief surging to the front.

I could stop the sorrow. With the slightest nudge, I could mute her feelings so she didn't have to drown in them anymore. So I didn't.

There was already enough guilt over doing that once, and with the way Nico was watching me, he'd ruin things if he caught on.

"Dahlia's case was… complicated," I said.

"People say *it's complicated* when they think the answer will get them in trouble in some way."

I'd like to say I forgot Nico was with us, but the amount of resentment and doubt he radiated made that impossible.

I sighed. "The biggest reason I didn't offer this to

Dahlia is that she wouldn't have let me." Unlike the magic I was born with, the ability to influence people's emotions, this wasn't something I could lightly nudge in someone's direction. "It's not an easy process, and it has to be completed, or it can make things worse."

"But you can help me," Magnus said.

This was about to hurt. "Yes, but…"

"Might as well finish the thought. Dragging this out isn't helping anyone." Nico was irritated. Impatient.

How did I ever love this man? Why did I still? I kept my attention on Magnus. "Once we start, we can't stop. Tell me you understand that now, before I even explain."

She stared back, resolute. "You know I do."

"That's not enough. Not for this," I said. "What the heart feels and what the mind knows are not always the same, especially when it comes to consent—"

"Since when?" Nico muttered.

I wasn't going to spare him a glare. "Tell me you understand, Magnus."

She looked between the two of us, brows raised, and landed on me. "I understand. Once we start, we can't stop, or it could make things worse. What is it, and how does it work?"

"Do you remember when Ice Queen broke her

arm in hand-to-hand?" Real life examples were always better than metaphor or theory.

Magnus nodded. "She didn't tell anyone and it didn't heal right. They had to break it again and reset it."

Fucking assholes had known the girl's arm was broken, but it was all part of the tests those soldiers were subjected to. "Three main things keep you from accessing your power once it's awakened," I said. "A physical block, an emotional one, or a magical one. I can't always see which is the cause, but regardless, the cure is to break the connection and let it reconnect properly."

She nodded. "That makes sense. That's why stopping too soon can cause a problem."

She was smart. Stunning. Dangerous with that mind.

I adored it.

"Exactly. Like a bone, it has to be set properly for it to heal properly. Unlike Western medicine, this isn't a science. I may have to break multiple *bones* for the process to work, and it hurts just as much."

Magnus frowned. "Does it take as long to heal? Because I can't wait six to ten weeks between each break. I want those gods to suffer now."

There was the soldier.

"No. It only takes a few hours to a few days to heal. This is more of an endurance test." I had to be careful with this because if she was embracing the things she'd learned at TOM, especially when it came to suffering through pain, she'd push too hard.

"How do you know how to do this?" Nico asked. "This isn't a skill you had when we were together."

Because the prophecies of Urd said I'd lose my own godhood someday, and I'd spent a century or two learning how to get it back once it was gone. Every member of the TOM board was named in the prophecies. "How do you know how to use a phone? You learned."

Nico raised an eyebrow. "Right."

Doubt whispered into Magnus's heart, and she squashed it. She wanted this so badly, her need tasted like smooth, bitter chocolate. "I'm in. I'm saying it, so it counts. I'm in."

Nico stood with a disgusted huff. "You're going to let Bragi torture you."

"Success by any means necessary." Magnus didn't know what those words meant, but she thought she did.

"They brainwashed you well, didn't they?" Judgment and disgust spilled from Nico, cast in my direction.

Magnus wasn't having it, even if she couldn't name the emotions the way I could. "I may hate a lot of the aspects of my upbringing, but it made me who I am now. I'm going into this with my eyes wide open."

"Are you?" Nico countered. "Including whatever Bragi hasn't told you?"

Magnus glanced at me, her doubt swelling again.

"I'll tell you everything about this process. Every step of the way. I don't want you left in the dark on any of it." That was true.

Silence stretched between the three of us as she decided how much faith to give me. It didn't matter that I couldn't hear her thoughts. Centuries of feeling gave me the insight to recognize her current blend of emotion. She knew I was keeping things from her, but she was willing to risk the consequences to have what she wanted.

Her decision tinged the air before she spoke. "I'm still in," she said.

"I'm not going to watch this." Nico strode toward the door.

I was fine with that, with one exception. "You can't leave the property. We already discussed it, and doing so puts Magnus at risk."

He was annoyed. Pissed off. Willing to do an awful lot for a woman he just met. He faced us again. "Fine. I'll be in my room."

Magnus didn't want him to go, but she was committed to this decision.

Please don't let me regret this. I didn't know who I was praying to, since no one would hear me, but I tossed the request out into the ether just in case

there was some power higher than dragons to hear
my plea.

CHAPTER 8

MAGNUS

Bragi gave me a quick tour of the house, including where the kitchen was, told me to make myself at home, and suggested that when I dressed in the morning that I leave as much skin as possible exposed for our healing therapy.

"If we can't come and go, to get me clothes, I'll be wearing this or nothing," I said.

"There are clothes in the dresser. I grabbed you some things while you were recovering."

That was both convenient and creepy.

"I'll see you in the morning." Bragi left me alone for the night in my own temporary room. It was as nice as his was, furniture-wise, but it was plain. Beige patterned rug on hardwood. Pale blankets. Muted stain on the wooden dresser and desk.

But I was still alone with my thoughts. My sorrow. My confusion and frustration and rage.

I shouldn't care what Nico thought of my decision to move forward with *therapy*; I barely knew the guy. But there was a connection there. An invisible thread I felt tying me to him. I felt a similar tug to Bragi.

Then again, I'd sworn I had something like that with Vidar, and hey, fuck that guy. Though I wished now I never had.

And I felt a bond with Dahlia too. It wasn't romantic, but it was still love. I swore I felt it even now. A tug to her heart, that ran through every plane where beings existed. Maybe the bond ran through time and space, too, and that was why Dahlia's presence lingered in my soul the way it did. That feeling that if I turned around, I'd see her standing behind me.

Or that was how intense my grief was.

I pulled out a chair and sat, not sure what else to do. If I planned to stay, I'd decorate the place. Add some pink and black. Paint some chibis on the walls.

But this wasn't my home. It was a layover point until I ended the previous chapter of my life and started the next. This was the bookmark in my story, nothing more.

Being in this house by myself, knowing there were two other people here, was disconcerting. I wandered into the kitchen to find a fridge and pantry stocked with ingredients, but not much food.

Where was the ice cream? The frozen pizza? The instant noodles?

The flour and dried pasta and wine and frozen meat made me think either Bragi was cooking, bringing in a cook, or eating out a lot.

For a short while, after we walked away from TOM, Dahlia and I ate in a different city every week. We would hop a plane, charge it to the corporate account that chaos kept anyone from watching, and fly to a new continent whenever we wanted.

Wonderful. Now food reminded me of her. I grabbed an apple, took the most winding path I could to my room, and didn't encounter a single soul along the way.

It was a good thing I was tired. What were the odds I could sleep without dreaming again of Dahlia's and Fen's deaths?

There was no clock in the room, so I didn't know how long I slept, but my wish went unanswered and my nightmares remained consistent. Worst. Reruns. Ever.

Sleep sucked, and I wasn't doing it again unless I was so tired my brain didn't work.

I sifted through the dresser, seeing what kind of clothing I had. A lot of racerback sports bras and backless tops. He'd shopped specifically to accommodate my wings. Touching. Bothersome that it was necessary. Still creepy that he nailed my size and style so perfectly.

I hope he fixed my wings first, because I had no desire to get used to leaving my back exposed and sleeping on my side.

If I walked into this thing naked, how would Bragi react? Could I get a different kind of distraction from my thoughts and feelings? The way he watched me—the things he offered and had done for me—he was interested in more than making sure I had a nice day. Sex was an incredible release and distraction, and I bet he could teach me some tricks I'd never seen in the bedroom.

I'd start with a sports bra and sweat shorts instead.

He knocked on my door moments after I finished dressing, saving me from spending much more time with my thoughts and schemes to escape them. The way he dragged his gaze over me sent heat and an intense need racing over me, along with an intense need to escape into the kind of fuck that blanked my mind.

"Are you ready?" Bragi's tone was polite and nothing else.

As ready as I could be. "Yes."

"Follow me."

I did. Down the hallway, past the library and sitting room, and toward the kitchen. With each step, my anticipation notched higher. Each millimeter closer to what waited for me. *Torture.* Did he feel what I was radiating? Dread mixed with a morbid curiosity combined with a twisted sort of need? I could suppress all of that physically—I was one hell of a poker player—but there was no hiding my emotions from him.

As I fully realized the thought, I suddenly felt more exposed than if I'd decided to do this naked. An involuntary shudder ran through me, though I wasn't sure if it was fear or need.

Both, perhaps.

We stepped up to a door before the kitchen that I hadn't noticed last night. It was unlike me to miss a door, so when had he materialized it or unhidden it?

Bragi pushed through and I followed, expecting to step into some sort of room with training pads or workout equipment. My adrenaline surged. It was too bright for me to see. Would I have to fight? Run? Fuck my way out of the situation?

As my eyes adjusted, green swam into view. Not army green, but the bright, vibrant color of clover. We were in a forest clearing that was distinctly not part of the house. The faint scent of flowers hung in the air, and a light breeze rustled through trees, causing the shadows and sunlight to dance around us.

For a moment, I forgot to breathe, it was so beautiful.

A wooden picnic table sat in the middle of it all —the sort with attached benches—looking out of place amid the scene.

Bragi stepped next to me. "This will be exactly what I described yesterday. I'll sever connections and let them heal again, but it will all happen quickly. Seconds, maybe minutes, but not longer."

"How will that work if my missing Valkyrie healing is part of the issue?"

"This isn't like normal healing magic. I'll put a kind of cast around the break." He furrowed his brow, then relaxed his face. "Like soldering connections back together."

I appreciated him reaching for an analogy I'd understand, but the comparison was still lacking. "Solder leaves waste. A bulge where it drops."

"Not if the person doing the work is good at it."

"*Exceptionally* good at it. A master."

Bragi sighed. "I've had a lot of practice."

"On who?" The answer sat like a pit in my gut, and I wanted to be wrong.

"Potentials."

I wasn't. The reality of what he was saying sank in. He'd tortured enough potentials to consider himself an expert at it, in the name of unlocking their magic. "With their permission, like you got from me."

"Eventually," he said.

Fuck.

"Look at me." Bragi stepped into my eyeline, but didn't make contact. "I'm being honest with you about this because you deserve the truth. I'm not that person anymore, but like you said yesterday, I won't pretend those things aren't in my past."

I'd known he did shitty things, and I said I was pursuing my path by any means necessary. I knew this Bragi. He wasn't the only one with death in his past. Fenrir for instance, and Dahlia loved him.

The reminder of who I was doing this for solidified my resolve. "Let's get started."

MAGNUS

Bragi sat on the table, his feet on a bench. "Sit between my legs, back to me."

Sitting with my back to anyone was a terrifying prospect, especially in my current condition. I'd slept unconscious in his bed for a week though, so in theory I'd be okay. Taking a mental deep breath, I complied.

I couldn't hide my sharp inhale when he grazed his fingertips down my neck to rest on my shoulders.

"Are you all right?" he asked, as if he couldn't feel the desire whispering through me.

How many nights had I fantasized about his touch when I was in school? I'd slept with some of the other gods. While the notion turned my stomach now, I'd fucked Vidar more than once. "I'm good," I said.

"You need to relax. That's key for what we're

going to do. Like stretching before you work out, so you don't tear muscle."

"Easier said than done." My chuckle was tight.

Bragi pressed his thumbs into the muscle where my back met my neck, and kneaded lightly.

My groan wouldn't be suppressed.

"Focus on the sounds outside of your heart. On my touch." Bragi's voice was low and soothing. "Don't try to stop yourself from thinking, but don't hold onto any of those thoughts. Let them go and return to focusing on the external."

As he talked, he glided his hands along my shoulders, to the blades, down my spine, between my wings, massaging and talking me through a guided meditation.

I'd always been horrible at this, but it never came with the kind of touch I craved. The problem was, every time relaxation flitted in, so did guilt and grief and thoughts of Dahlia. I tried not to hold on, to release it all, but I didn't want to. I needed to remember how much this hurt.

Bragi's almost imperceptible sigh made me feel like I'd failed some sort of test. "It's okay. Don't do that," he said.

"Don't feel?"

He rested his hands on my shoulders again, thumbs tracing tiny circles over my skin. "Don't feel bad about feeling."

Yeah. Right.

"It'll get easier as we go on," he said. "For now, we begin. Stop me at any point if it becomes too much."

I swallowed my snort of disbelief, but my, "I won't," slipped out.

"You will, or we don't move forward."

The way he was driving this point of *it's going to hurt* home was starting to make me nervous. "Okay. I'll stop you if it becomes too much."

"Good girl." His voice was so quiet, it blended with the trickle of a nearby stream.

I heard it loud and clear regardless. Could he hear me get a girl boner?

The way he glided his fingers along my back and around the edges of my feathers made my pulse race. The first strands of pain were like plucking hairs—a momentary sting that faded instantly. Sometimes the sensation was in my body, then my heart, and finally it was a tug I couldn't quite feel. Like yanking on skin that had been numbed with a local anesthetic.

This wasn't even as bad as waxing my legs. Talk about over-hyped. The combination of faint pain and a delicate touch, probably with a hint of his magic mixed in, sent tingles spilling through me. Along my nerve endings, in my nipples, and between my legs.

He had to be feeling what I was. Or was this entire experience physical? I'd been trained to numb myself enough to get through any task, and *goddess* I wanted to do that now. Ignore all of my emotion and only focus on his touch.

"How are you holding up?" Bragi asked, his voice thicker than it should be.

More turned on than I expected to be. Desperate for a way to escape my own grief for a short while. Eager for vengeance. "Fine."

"Now the pain starts."

Yeah, okay.

There was a pause in his ministrations, and then I felt a heavy pressure along the edge of my spine, like a knife cutting skin, despite there being no blade. As the weight lifted, the pain sank in. A sharp sting that didn't fade the way the others had.

It hurt. It made me think of danger. It kicked up my adrenaline, and I braced myself for more.

The preparedness wasn't enough to stop what came next from hurting. With each invisible slice, it ached more, until I was gritting my teeth and squeezing my eyes shut to fight the tears.

I was supposed to stop him when it was too much, but we weren't there yet.

Bragi traced a fingernail along the edge of one of my wings, and my entire shoulder blade shattered into a million pieces, clenched in a non-existent fist.

A scream wrenched from my throat, and I couldn't stop it, despite thinking through the agony. This wasn't real. My bones weren't actually broken.

But *fuck* it felt like a portion of me was being ground to dust.

"We're done for now." Bragi spoke with a finality that left no room for argument.

Not that I had the strength to protest.

He escorted me back to my room, not saying anything until we arrived. "Get as much rest as you can. We can go again when the pain stops. Keep in mind, I'll know if you're lying about that."

I gritted my teeth and nodded. The instant he was gone, I collapsed into bed and sleep consumed me. My dreams were mostly of Dahlia dying, but they were dotted with new images too. I chased the visions of pleasure, the ones where Bragi, sometimes Nico, played my body like an instrument until my screams were the musical sound of pleasure.

And guilt consumed me for daring to think such a thing.

When I woke up, I was soaked in sweat and desire. During my training, sex had been an outlet. We were all taught that as Nobles—fucking wasn't about love. It was either to gather information, or like most physical activities, to find release.

The pain was gone, and while my mind wasn't refreshed, my body was ready for more. Since I didn't have an outlet and my fingers didn't feel like a reasonable substitute, I showered, pulled on a fresh set of nearly nothing, and sought out Bragi.

For the next week, two to three times a day, we

repeated the process. Each time as we finished, my frustration was more potent as I collapsed in my bed. I hadn't made any progress. My powers were still out of reach.

The only thing that changed was my dreams grew more erotic. As I slept, I swore I could feel one man or the other, sometimes both, lying in bed with me, their hands gliding over my bare skin and coaxing me to orgasms that mingled with my pain and exhaustion to mute my grief.

And each time I woke up, we started the cycle all over again.

I sat between Bragi's legs as he glided a light touch over my skin. We were in the *mild pain* part of the process. He hit different points every session, and was currently trailing along my neck. It was easy to lose myself in this. To picture that his lips would follow. That the sharp stings would be soothed away, and then replaced with a strong bite.

While he fractured and healed a hundred tiny pathways along my jaw, I was picturing his hands slipping lower. Under my bra, to cup my breasts and tease my nipples.

"Can you leash that?" Bragi's strained request yanked me from the blooming fantasy.

He meant my lust. I probably could, but I needed *something*. "No."

His hands dropped away. "We're done for now."

"Good." I spun on the bench, putting me at eye-level with his stomach, and tilted my head up to see him. There was no point in trying to hide my frustrated desire. "Then we can do something else." It would be so easy to slide my hands up the inside of his thighs. To tease his cock through his trousers until he was hard... If he wasn't already.

Bragi shook his head, and dropped onto the bench next to me. "No," he mimicked my earlier answer.

"I'll be doing something else regardless. I don't cease to exist just because you see me to my room." I turned in my seat again and straddled the bench.

He put himself in a similar position to face me, his knees outside of mine, pinning me in place. As he searched my face, he rested a hand at the base of my neck. When he yanked my hair, there was no question that the sensation was physical. Real.

So much better than an ethereal pain that wasn't solving any problems.

He worked his jaw, but no sound came out. If I spoke, if I demanded or coaxed or begged, would it ruin the moment. I was so desperate for his touch that need overrode the lingering aches of therapy.

Bragi tilted his head and drew me closer. His breath was hot on my skin and my lips tingled for the tiniest taste. He was near enough I felt his heat.

A whimper slipped from my throat.

He let go of me with a gasp, and stood, putting more than a meter between us in an instant. "We're done," he said with such finality that there was no questioning it.

Fine. I whirled away and headed into the house. Humiliation and frustration flowed through me as I stalked back to my room. What was I thinking?

That I was really fucking horny. That I needed to claw my way out of my own head. That I just wanted to be held and share an orgasm or two with another living being and be told everything was going to be okay, even if it wasn't.

Was that so wrong?

"Magnus?" Nico's voice yanked me to a stop as I passed the library.

I turned to see him in the same spot as the first day I came in here. The way he watched me from the loveseat made my breath catch.

"Your wings," he said.

What about them? I flexed them and wrapped them around me, so I could see the ends. Hope fluttered in my chest. They weren't scorched anymore. They were the same vibrant auburn as my hair, the way they were supposed to be.

I stepped in front of the nearest mirror—Bragi didn't own a single clock that I'd seen, but he had plenty of ways to look at himself—and my gasp was more surprise than desire this time. My wings were healed. As I flexed them, they were glorious, with a wide span, and nearly shone even in the muted indoor lighting.

I couldn't withdraw them, but this was a change. What we were doing was working.

"*Fuck* you're gorgeous." Nico's awe mingled with mine, and I turned to find him watching me with open desire.

CHAPTER 10

NICODEMUS

Watching Magnus with her wings spread, natural curls framing her flushed face, I was captivated.

"You're pretty sexy yourself." Her tone was playful, but a darker note lay underneath.

"Where are you going in such a huff?" I hadn't meant to interrupt her determined journey, but her name had slipped out before I could stop myself.

She shook her head. "Back to my room to wallow in humiliation."

"Why?" It was difficult to imagine any of that applying to her.

Magnus huffed and clucked. "Because I just threw myself at Bragi, and he made it quite clear what I wanted wasn't happening."

That didn't sound right. Perhaps the terminology was different than I remembered? Sometimes the centuries caught up with me and I lost track of modern slang. "To be clear, what was it you wanted?"

"Sex."

That was pretty clear. Her bluntness was both surprising and refreshing.

"What have you been up to?" She moved closer but didn't sit.

We were changing the subject. Probably for the best, though I was considering offering my services if she still wanted sex. "Reading. Trying not to think about what you may or may not be feeling when the two of you vanish through that door." Wondering how long it had been since I felt the kind of drive that was consuming her to be tortured every few hours.

"Huh. That sounds a lot like what I've been doing, but without the reading. We have so much in common." Her retort was almost teasing.

"Hence the desire for sex?" I asked.

If she was surprised by my reply, it didn't show. "Yes."

I stood, my body all-but touching hers, and she didn't step back. "I'd be happy to act as a stand-in."

"You volunteer as tribute?" Magnus almost smiled.

"That's one way to put it. If you think you can handle the substitution."

"I'm not sure if you're being arrogant or dismissive of yourself, but being with you hardly sounds like settling."

Once upon a time, I would've sung praises about Bragi as a lover from the highest hills. "It's not settling in any way." I cupped her face and stroked a thumb along her cheek. "Is that a *yes*?"

"That's a *fuck yes*. As in, *fuck me please*." Her directness was different from what I was used to.

I quite liked it. I kissed her softly, not trusting myself to dive in headfirst. The spark that flowed between us zinged all the way into my toes, and in that instant, I was done for. I slid my hand to the back of her neck, gripping tight, and deepened the kiss.

The way she pressed back, her tongue wrestling with mine and her groans mingling with mine, was intoxicating. Heat enveloped us in a way I'd never experienced, and I was a being who could surround myself with flame.

Magnus gripped my shirt in her fists and nudged me back with her full body. We half-stumbled into the loveseat, and then she was straddling my legs.

Her clothing showed as much skin as it covered, and I memorized the smooth, soft texture over muscle honed by years of training, as I dragged my fingers down her sides, brushing her wings before gripping her thighs and pulling her into me.

Magnus glided her fingers down the front of my shirt, deftly undoing each button she encountered.

I didn't have the patience to wait for her to finish, and I ripped the fabric open, popping the last few buttons off and sending them flying.

Her giggle was delight tinged with sorrow, and the dichotomy of the sound made my heart ache. She dipped her head to kiss along my bare chest, grinding against my cock with each shift of her body.

There was so much to explore, and I didn't have the patience for any of it. I needed more of her, *now*. I raised her head again, and claimed her mouth in a hungry kiss before nipping at her chin. Shoving her bra up to expose her breasts, so I could suckle and feast.

She tasted incredible. Like life and love and pain and everlasting death—the kind that meant there was more after this life—and I swore there was a hint of bitter chocolate and cinnamon on her skin.

Magnus was hunger and I was desperation and we fed each other's frenzied grind to get closer. Her heat pressed into my erection, teasing through too many layers of fabric, while I alternated which of her breasts I gave attention to. She worked her hips until I thought my cock might drill a hole in my pants, to get to her.

I wedged my fingers between us. The angle was awkward as I teased her through her shorts and panties, and I didn't care. She reached down and yanked the fabric aside, exposing herself.

The instant my fingers brushed her wetness, she dug her nails into my arms with a drawn-out moan. She slipped easily against my touch, and I teased her swollen clit while I sucked and bit her nipples.

With each shift of her hips, her breathing grew more punctuated. The weight of her body against me felt more needy. She came with a drawn-out cry that sang to my soul, digging her fingers into my shoulders and working her hips as if her life depended on it.

"It's not enough." The words rasped from her throat.

She was right—it wasn't.

I had no idea how I got my zipper down, but I managed to work my cock free. When I slid inside her tight, wet pussy, I let out a long *fuuuuck*.

Magnus laughed.

And then I was holding onto her hips like a lifeline in a storm, slamming inside her. Finding the rhythm between us as she bounced in my lap. She fingered herself while she rode me.

The world around us fell away, and the only thing I saw was her. The only thing I smelled or tasted was her. Her gasps as she hovered near another climax were life's soundtrack and the way she clenched around me when she came was desire given a physical form.

I couldn't hold back any longer. I spilled inside

her, grunting and hammering until we were both spent.

As Magnus slowed to a stop, our pants for breath came in unison. She leaned the rest of her weight into me and rested her forehead on my shoulder.

I tilted my head to rest against hers and my gaze fell on the open library doorway. Not that it mattered here—Bragi would feel us regardless and there was no staff to walk in on us. However, the fact that I'd never considered where we were before we started was a good indicator of how far gone I was for this woman.

Who I barely knew.

A vision from my dreams who was so much more in real life.

They were fucking in my house.

I took Magnus in when she needed it. I invited Nico to be a guest.

And their thanks was the two of them fucking where it was impossible for me to ignore it.

Did I have a right to be jealous? Absolutely not. There were so many things I didn't have the right to do, like take advantage of Magnus's proposition during therapy.

Did knowing that stop me from seething with envy? Absolutely not.

If I were in a more rational frame of mind, I'd be able to shrug off my reaction, but with their lust spilling over everything and mingling with my own desire, it was all I could do to not join them.

I couldn't do that though. As much as my body ached to know what it felt like to be with Magnus, I wouldn't cross that line. Knowing how long she'd been drawn to me. How fragile her defenses were at this moment. The first day she turned her lust in my direction, back when neither of us had decided to walk away from TOM, I promised myself I wouldn't take advantage of her vulnerabilities.

Today, in the clearing, she was an exposed nerve, and I was terrified that if I touched her, if my lips met hers, I wouldn't be able to stop myself from nudging. Enough emotion to make her feel better. A whisper of something to increase her desire. A topping of suggestion that would keep her coming back for more.

I wouldn't do that to her.

Instead, I stood in my kitchen, letting Magnus's and Nico's need spill over me, until I was willingly drowning in their lust.

As her desire peaked, I freed my cock and stroked, squeezing so hard the shaft ached. Her desperation didn't fade, and his roared. The blend of twin flames filled me with memories of what I'd lost and what I'd never had, until I thought my chest might burst.

When Magnus's pleasure hit a climax again, I was yanking my dick so hard my entire body jerked.

Nico's orgasm sent me tumbling over the edge, and I came hard, splattering the cupboard and floor with cum, grunting from both physical exertion and emotional, and dropping to my knees when my legs refused to support me.

How much longer could I keep this up?

As long as Magnus needed me to.

I cleaned up my mess and retired to my room to grab a few hours of sleep.

Magnus's approach woke me. She wasn't bleeding emotion the way she had been, and instead had wrapped her feelings in a block of ice and buried them deep in her chest.

They weren't gone, and if I tried I could pluck out every one, but this made it easier for me to ignore them as well. Her training had served her.

When she knocked, I forced alertness and my own sense of calm through my veins and answered.

"I'd like to go again. I'll behave," she said.

A new flash of color drew my eye. "Your wings."

She nodded. "It's working. Thank you for everything you've done so far. I'd like to go again. Please." She was the perfect picture of control. Hel would've been so proud, and that was the last thing I was going to tell Magnus.

"All right." I walked with her toward the doorway, keeping as much distance as was possible in the hallway.

Nico was waiting for us when we arrived, and Magnus's surprise flickered before she buried it again. He kicked away from the wall. "I'd like to go with you, if that won't interfere."

My smile was tight. "I thought you didn't want to watch this."

"I don't. However, I'd like to see the results, and there are other things I'd like to keep an eye on." The way he studied Magnus was brazen and obvious.

She was still blanketing her response.

Terrifying and beautiful.

We stepped through the doorway into the clearing. This wasn't a random spot I'd created out of thin air, though what I could do with that kind of power. It was a clearing a few kilometers from where my house currently resided in the fae world.

I was strong enough to keep us separate from the rest of the realm, though. We could see the scenery and nature, but other living beings—animals, people, gods —couldn't see us and we wouldn't see them. Or rather, Magnus and Nico wouldn't. I kept myself aware of the surroundings for her safety, in case there was something out there I couldn't hide us from after all.

Though Magnus no longer needed my disclaimers about the process, I had rules to lay down for Nico. "You may watch," I told him. "But do not interfere. While we're doing this, I don't care what you see or feel, do *not* interrupt. If you do, you could make this far worse."

He was concerned. "How bad will it get?"

"I scream sometimes," Magnus said. "But if you can't follow the rules, you'll need to leave."

She wanted this to work so badly. Maybe she did understand *no matter the cost.*

Nico settled near a patch of clover and crossed his legs. "I won't interfere. No matter how bad it gets."

Magnus and I worked through the routine. Meditation. Relaxation. Pain.

I was glad she could see the progress in her wings, because I felt it. Every time I restored another pathway, more of her magic opened up. It was just so badly damaged that it was taking work. Since most of her Valkyrie was locked away, results would most likely happen in stuttered bursts rather than in a gradual flow.

It was necessary for me to ignore the attraction that surged inside with every touch, especially after yesterday. I barely had focus for anything but working on her and ignoring how my body responded, and the entire affair was draining.

But I was close. I felt another surge near the surface. If I could restore a few more connections—

"Do you feel that?"

I snapped from my mini trance and shot a glare at Nico. "I told you not to interrupt."

He stared back, confused. "I didn't."

"He didn't," Magnus said.

Then who—?

"I do. What is it?"

The first voice had been a man's. This one was a woman's. No, not just any woman.

Dahlia.

I clenched my jaw, and turned my attention outside my magic bubble.

"Bragi?" Magnus sounded concerned.

I held up a finger, silencing her, and extended my senses.

"It's so familiar," Gwydion said. *"I can't quite reach it."*

"It's... Magnus?" Dahlia was so sad.

Great. I had one of them on either side of me. Could they feel each other? *Fuck.* No one had a connection like that, especially if they weren't related.

"Are you sure?" Frey was trying to be kind, but he'd heard this from Dahlia more than once recently. He thought she was missing her sister. I felt all of that spilling from him as he answered her.

The women's connection was stronger than anyone realized. Double fuck. The three of them were standing so close, if my shield fell, they'd see us. Magnus would see them.

Vidar would destroy them both.

"Are you all right?" Magnus asked.

I wanted to break through that next series of connections in her. Push her one step closer to healing. If I didn't get her out of here now, everything would fall apart.

"We need to go," I said. "Now."

Nico opened his mouth to argue, but Magnus was already on her feet and ready.

She was so well trained.

Within seconds, we were back in my house, and I had severed the connection to the clearing. If anyone opened the door, they'd find a broom closet.

"What was that?" Magnus asked.

"It wasn't safe there anymore." I hated the lie. I wanted to tell her the truth, but it wasn't an option. "You're not ready to fight."

Her frustration surged, and her emotions were the equivalent of a temper-tantrum. She still hid it well, though. "Soon."

I nodded. "Yes. Soon."

CHAPTER 12

NICODEMUS

It was clear to me that Bragi's hasty retreat from the clearing was a lie. Or rather, his reasons for it were. I didn't know what he was hiding, but I wasn't surprised at the deception.

"Is that it? We're done for now?" Magnus sounded disappointed as the three of us stood in the hallway.

Bragi frowned. "That spot is special. As in, I set it up specifically for this."

"Set it up to keep her safe? Because obviously that didn't work." I wasn't sure what to ask to get him to reveal his secrets, but I was willing to prod from different angles to figure it out.

"She's safe, isn't she? And no. The environment there is different, so I added to it."

Magnus waved her arms and spread her wings to their full span, taking up a large length of walkway.

"Hi, I'm right here and I have a name. Are you telling me I have to go hide in my room until *it's safe*? Because spoiler alert—that's getting old."

"I'm happy for your company. I'd rather you don't hide," I said. I didn't blame her for being disappointed that they didn't finish their session, but I was grateful they hadn't gotten to the *screaming in pain* part of things. After last night with Magnus, I was going to be that possessive guy. Not because I'd stuck my dick in her, but she had a vulnerability that was hard to describe.

What I saw in her... It was probably the same thing Bragi did and I wasn't letting him or anyone break that in her.

"You're supposed to heal and recover after each session, Magnus." Bragi was focused on her.

She wrinkled her nose. "Which I don't need to do at this time. Can we order pizza?"

"What? *No.*" The intensity of Bragi's disbelief was almost amusing.

Magnus folded her wings down, and leaned against a nearby wall with a huff. "Did you know that you only have ingredients in your house?"

"And you know how to cook," Bragi said.

She rolled her eyes. "That doesn't mean I want to do it all the time. How often do you cook?"

"Why pizza?" As entertaining as this was, I didn't want to choose between sacrificing tears and letting Bragi have an aneurysm.

Magnus faltered. "I don't know. I just... have a craving."

I loved to cook if I had an appreciative audience, and I had been itching to try out Bragi's kitchen. "I've got this. Follow me."

Magnus kicked away from the wall without hesitation, but what surprised me was that Bragi followed as well. In the kitchen, I pointed to one of the stools by the center island. "Sit." I told Magnus.

She complied with a shrug.

Bragi watched, expression blank, his arms crossed.

Okay.

There was silence while I rummaged in the fridge and pantry for what I needed. I set a cutting board in front of Magnus, along with a knife, tomatoes, onions, and green peppers. "Will you dice these?"

"Sure." She twirled the blade handle between her fingers effortlessly. An impressive sight, given it wasn't weighted for anything beyond the most basic kitchen use.

I set to work making the dough.

"What can I do?" Now Bragi wanted to participate.

I shook my head. "Go rest and recuperate? Somewhere else?"

He finally took a seat. "I'm good here."

"So, what are you reading?" Magnus asked as we worked.

"Right now? Nothing," I teased.

One corner of her mouth tugged up. "No, not right now. You sit in the library all day, and you have a different book every time I see you. What kind of tales catch your eye?"

"Mostly modern fantasy." I'd moved on from *The Iliad* and *The Odyssey* ages ago.

Magnus sliced through a tomato like she was being timed, and scraped the little squares into one of the bowls I'd given her. "Like *Harry Potter*? *Game of Thrones*?" She sounded intrigued.

Ah. I'd fallen out of touch with the timeline again. "Like *Alice in Wonderland* and *The Hobbit*."

Bragi rolled his eyes. Because of course he did. Once upon a time, we'd pored over volumes together. Spent hours and days wrapped in each other, reading aloud about made-up worlds. If I wasn't careful, I'd start to miss those days.

When he glanced at me with one raised eyebrow, I realized my feelings were leaking. Best keep an eye on that. "I was surprised to see them in *your* library, Bragi."

"I own most every book I've ever read."

"I didn't see anything newer in there." Magnus made quick work of the remaining tomatoes, and pushed me the bowl.

"Ebooks," Bragi said. "Even a god who can create small pockets of reality runs out of shelf space."

I didn't care for anything electronic. "What do you do when the batteries die?"

"Plug it in and recharge it." The *well that's a dumb question* was clear in Magnus's retort. "I can't believe you both read fantasy."

"I wouldn't have pegged you as a literary snob." The dough was mixed, so I set it aside to let it rest, and moved onto other steps. There was a lot more she didn't know that she wouldn't believe.

Magnus shook her head. "I'm not—give me aliens and androids any day. But real-life magic is nothing like book magic. You know what actually exists. How can you read about the made-up stuff?"

"Real life spaceships are nothing like book space-ships." Bragi looked between the two of us, furrowed his brow, and walked to the fridge. "*I* can't believe you forgot the meat."

Magnus snorted. "I promise you he didn't."

Bragi's scowl was worth a million dollars. He pulled a package of sausage from the freezer, and tossed it onto the counter in front of me.

He had to be jealous of what happened yester-day. I'd bet that same million on that. Jealous that I had her, or did the feeling go both ways? Once upon a time, he would've joined me, regardless of who I was with. I didn't try to hide anything this time, as I looked him over. He was as stunning as he'd ever been, and in this casual setting, it was easy to remember all the good things.

I mentally cleared my throat and moved back to the conversation. "It's the books that get magic right that you need to be scared of. Or rather, the authors of said books."

"Why?" Magnus finished dicing, and went to wash her hands.

"It means whoever wrote them isn't afraid of sharing their secrets. Which almost always means—"

"Crazy or powerful." I finished Bragi's thought.

He nodded. "Or both."

Leaning back against the sink, her hands on the counter behind her, Magnus studied us. "Who gets it right?"

"No one you've heard of," I said. Their books tended to be seen as *unrealistic* and *hard to follow* and languished in obscurity. I kneaded the dough, then started stretching it out.

As I worked, Bragi grabbed the olive oil from a cupboard I hadn't seen, and tossed the tomatoes with it. He added in some garlic and fresh oregano as he worked. "Tolkien is a god."

"Wow." Magnus's disbelief was tangible. "Fanboy much?"

I wasn't familiar with the slang, but I could translate, given the context, and it made me laugh. "No. Literally. He lives on an unmapped island in the South Pacific, thriving on the worship of millions and rather pleased with himself that he redefined reality and people eat it up." I arranged the dough in a mostly-circle on a giant wooden spatula.

"The names he's gone by over the centuries." Bragi spread the tomato mixture evenly over the dough.

Working like this with him came so easily. The rhythm was still there between us, after all this time.

Magnus nudged the remaining ingredients toward us. "You're both full of shit. What names?"

"Homer. Shakespeare." I finished covering the pizza with vegetables and meat.

"Martin." Bragi sounded disgusted.

Magnus grinned. "Not a fan? Of the man or just the new books? Or did you skip them in favor of the TV show? Because that was your mistake."

The look Bragi gave her was pure offense. "*Never* skip the book in favor of the adaptation. No matter the century or the technology." He topped the pizza with thick slices of mozzarella.

I'd missed this—him—so much, and I hated to admit it, but I also couldn't lie to myself about it. I slid the pizza into the oven, on top of a waiting stone, and turned to see Bragi watching me with something that almost looked like regret. He turned away when my gaze met his.

I gestured toward him. "Magnus, meet C.S.

Lewis." One of the many names Bragi had written under over the centuries.

The bastard actually blushed. "She didn't need to know that."

"No shit. Jesus allegory lion is yours?"

Bragi cringed. "*Thor* allegory."

"*Oh.*" Magnus's entire expression was a kind of joy I didn't know if I'd ever get to see in her. "Are you HG Wells? Do you know him?"

"I am not. *Not* a god. Though I'm sure the dragons would love to have claimed he was one of them."

At the word *dragon* Magnus's face fell.

"I'm sorry." Bragi sounded sincere. "I didn't mean to remind you—"

"It's okay. I'm okay." Her voice was tight. "The doorway in the hall... Narnia?"

"Tweaked version of reality, yes," Bragi said.

Perhaps I could distract her a little. "Lewis Carroll was visiting once and accidentally stumbled through one of the doorways that led to the fae realm."

Magnus's eyes grew wide. "No. Shit."

"I thought if I stuck it in a mirror, it would stay hidden." Bragi huffed a sigh. "Oops. Oh, and Mary Shelley..."

I let out a long whistle. "You would've liked her. Mortal. Brilliant. Fortunate she didn't have to know most of those pompous asses." And the orgies...

Watching Bragi seduce someone. The intensity he radiated just from being himself.

Letting him seduce me...

A lump bubbled up in my chest.

"This all makes so much sense." Magnus's joy was back. Not as bright as before, but this was better than sadness. "You're C.S. Lewis. Fucking hell, that's kind of sexy."

My jealousy surged.

"Only kind of?" Bragi must have noticed, but he was keeping his own reaction to himself.

Magnus grinned. "I mean, it's not like you're Tolkien."

Bragi scowled.

I laughed.

"I ought to spank you for that," Bragi said.

She hopped from her stool and stuck her ass in the air. "Promises, promises."

I'd watch that again and again. Magnus with two sets of flushed cheeks, bent over Bragi's knee. "Pizza!" It wasn't quite done, but fuck if I didn't need the distraction.

CHAPTER 13

MAGNUS

Can we order pizza?

What a childish thing to say. But it had just slipped out. In the clearing, right before Bragi made us leave, I felt a sense of peace like I hadn't had in a week. I swore Dahlia was *right there* next to me.

It was ridiculous and I knew it, but believing it made my heart relax and just for tonight, I wanted to remember what it was like when she was here. Which meant ordering pizza and being intentionally dumb.

What I was doing now wasn't quite the same—leave it to a couple of ancient gods to fuck up a modern tradition—but the fact that they made it different also made it okay. I still had my Dahlia memories and these were similar but wouldn't feel like a forced replacement.

The pizza on the plate Nico set in front of me didn't look like any pizza I'd ever had in any country, but it looked amazing. He and Bragi made themselves comfortable on either side of me at the high bar on the island, and I swore I felt the sparks passing through me.

I'd wondered since I woke up what brought two men together with so much obvious animosity between them. After watching them work together, the ease with which they talked when they let down their defenses, the shared history and looks, the chemistry...

They'd been lovers.

"Who broke whose heart?" I could wait for the information to come out, or try to subtly work it out of them, but Bragi would feel me being sneaky and being direct had served me well so far.

The heavy silence that settled in the room indicated I'd just broken my streak. I was about to take the question back when Bragi spoke.

"It was my fault."

That explained Nico's animosity.

"Any chance that you're friends again and you want to kiss and make up?" I kept my tone playful. I liked watching boys kiss boys as much as the next girl, and these were pretty boys. Did I mention the sparks? And if they happened to trap me between them—

"No." Nico's clipped answer sent any ideas I had crashing into a brick wall.

Alrighty then. I took a big bite of pizza and focused on savoring the flavors rather than the atmosphere around me. I swallowed. "Food's good."

"Thank you." The edge was gone from Nico's voice, but so was any other hint of emotion.

Awkward.

The pizza really was delicious though. We ate in silence.

"I regret what I did, every fucking day," Bragi said quietly. "That's tens of thousands of days of regret."

"You should've considered that before you did it."

Nico's retort prickled over me, tugging on my own regrets. "That's not fair." My retort popped out, and both men looked at me with shock. "Whatever it was, if it was serious enough to drive this kind of wedge between you, I doubt it was done without thought. People are allowed to make mistakes, and when we do, we can spend ages beating ourselves up over it. If you're not even going to give him a chance to make things better, after all this time..."

Then what chance did I have to atone for the things I'd done? Like going back to TOM, working for Vidar, after Dahlia and I swore we were done. Then later, getting her killed, instead of saving one of the men she loved.

"This isn't as simple as you think," Nico said.

I wouldn't be condescended to. "It never is. Nothing he did can be worse than—"

The heat of his gaze bored into the side of my head, and I focused on my food. This wasn't supposed to be about me. "Than what?" Nico asked.

I didn't want to talk about this. We were having such a good night.

"He's right." Bragi saved me. "I guarantee that nothing you've done compares. Even if you want to argue the moral—or immoral—severity of our different actions, I still acted inexcusably."

"What did you do?" I twisted my head to the side to glance at him.

He stared up at the ceiling, then down at his plate with a heavy sigh. "I made him love me."

I didn't understand. Or rather, an inkling in the back of my mind was starting to grasp Bragi's meaning, but I was terrified of what I'd find if I tugged and unraveled. I had to know, though. "How?"

"To be fair, I did fall on my own." Nico's voice was quiet. "I met a man who was witty and creative and an incredible fucking lover, and I was hooked."

"Until I fucked things up." Bragi pushed his plate away. "I don't even remember now what the fight was about."

I glanced at Nico, who shook his head. "I don't either."

Bragi's chuckle was strained. "He was furious,

though. Screaming. Inconsolable. And I just wanted him to listen."

"I would have. I needed to get it out of my system, and then I always calmed down after," Nico said.

"I couldn't wait, so I influenced his emotions. I sent a whisper of calm through him, to make him stop. Fuck, I still regret that day."

There was the reality I was trying to ignore. I knew Bragi was capable of that—of making people feel whatever emotions he needed to—but I tried not to put a lot of thought into how it could be used to manipulate. "But it was just that once, wasn't it?"

"With him, yes," Bragi said.

Nico grabbed our now-empty plates and carried them to the sink. "So you say."

"I do say. To this day, I swear to you, I only did it to you the once." Bragi moved to a different side of the kitchen, and grabbed a bottle of wine from a rack of them in a wine fridge. He plucked three glasses from the display hanging from the bottom of the cabinet above.

I was processing the ramifications of this news. "It's not like you can make people act against their will, right? You couldn't force Nico to forgive you, to love you, unless he already wanted to."

Nico's cough was a throat-clearing sound of skepticism.

Bragi pulled the cork from the wine bottle with

his bare hands. A deftly executed *pop* that would've impressed me if I wasn't preoccupied. He tilted the mouth over the first glass, and instead of pouring, took a long swallow directly from the bottle.

I didn't like the realization spilling through me. "You can't force people to do things they don't want to. Right?" I asked with more insistence.

Nico crossed the room to Bragi, took the wine from him, and indulged in his own drink. Ridiculous, since gods tended to metabolize alcohol quickly enough it wasn't getting them drunk. It looked more like they were drawing things out for drama's sake, and I didn't care for it.

"*Right?*" I raised my voice.

Bragi sighed. "You grew up with an entire campus full of strong-willed individuals. Vidar and Hel hand-picked Nobles from a stock of people who were intelligent, strong, and aggressive. Did you ever meet a Noble who did something they didn't want to?"

The question stuck in my mind, snagged on a loose nail of thought. Because the answer was *yes* but it was also *no*. "I saw them do things all the time that they didn't want to." But some of it served the individual's purpose and some of it...

My dinner churned in my gut. "That's what you did at TOM."

Bragi nodded. "I made students obey."

Oh, fuck. I wanted to storm from the room, but

my legs were rubber. The implications rolled through my mind. How far did he push? When Nobles were partnered with someone they couldn't stand? During seduction training?

"It's not a lasting suggestion," Bragi said. "I can't continue to make someone act a certain way, and if it's contrary to how they feel, the influence fades quickly. I can give enough of a nudge to get someone over a hump though."

I didn't want to ask my next question, but I had to. "How often with me?" Was that the reason I was attracted to him? No. He said he couldn't force me long-term. But now I was questioning...

"You're the reason I stopped," he said.

Oh, how sweet. The fact that his response didn't assure me meant that he wasn't manipulating me now, didn't it? "How often?"

"When I had to in order to keep you safe."

Was that why I'd trusted him when no one else did? Why I called him to help us find Vidar? Why I kept Frey from punishing him when Fen was shot? Was that why I wanted him so desperately last night? Was I about to be violently ill?

"No," Bragi said. "Whatever you're thinking, especially if it's about last night, I didn't."

Nico was being strangely quiet through all of this. He'd known. He'd gone through the same things I was now, hadn't he?

"So you can read minds now, too?" I tried to deflect, to give myself time to process.

Bragi shook his head. "No. But I can guess, based on what you're feeling. "

"It fucks with you, doesn't it?" Nico crossed the room and handed me the bottle.

"That's one way to put it." I accepted the offering and took a drink. If I wasn't currently magical, would I be the only one in the room who got drunk? Did I have enough control over my own feelings for it to matter?

Nico leaned in across from me, elbows on the counter, and looked me in the eye. "I'm not defending him, but I am trying to reassure you. It was how I knew he'd done it, because I remembered feeling the rage and then it was gone. It's not something that erases you." He furrowed his brow and hesitated. "Despite what he says, he didn't force me to love him. I fell on my own. The attraction is real and so is the desire."

"You know that for certain?" My doubt was so heavy. Gods and other immortals had lied to me and manipulated me since I was a teenager, yet I trusted Nico. And even Bragi. Even with this new information. How fucked up was I?

Nico nodded. "I know that for certain, because back then he begged me to stay. Begged me to forgive him. And it *ached* to walk away, because I do

—did love him. If he'd been creating that feeling in me, I would've stayed."

"I also don't have long-reaching influence. I can't call you on the phone and make you feel things. Though it's not necessary, touch works best. Far more effective than even just being in the same room as you," Bragi said.

"You were touching me last night." I didn't know what to think. What Nico said made sense, and the fact that I felt anything other than adoration and lust for Bragi at this moment must mean they were my own feelings. Unless he was projecting his self-loathing on me. But if he hated doing it, he was probably telling the truth about stopping, right?

Argh. I wouldn't lose myself in doubt. That was a path to insanity. I wouldn't let me kick myself off track. "And I was ready to ride you like a fucking horse."

"I'm not defending him, but I will guarantee Bragi didn't make you want him just so he could push you away and have to feel you fucking me." Nico reached up and slipped a leather cord over his head.

As he held it between us, the subtle light of the kitchen caught the stone suspected from the necklace, and it seemed to shimmer in a dozen colors at once, despite it not being bright enough in here. I didn't know why Bragi would make me want him if he wasn't going to take advantage of it, but these gods had fuck-up plans and ways of manipulating people. A lot of the things they did left me perplexed.

"I wouldn't have come when he called me if I didn't have this." Nico fitted the necklace onto me. It hung with a heavy weight over my heart. "It keeps me from being influenced."

But I still felt everything I had at the start of the conversation, including the desire and trust for Bragi. "Then why are you giving it to me?"

"Because I know what you're feeling. Because you're right that people make mistakes. Because you stood in the hallway with your fully healed wings spread and shimmered as brightly as the sun and that means he's actually healing you, so you can't stop now." Nico fingered the crystal one last time before letting his hand fall away.

"I give you my word that I didn't make you want me last night," Bragi said. "That I've never done that to you. But *fuck* you haunt my dreams, Magnus."

How was I supposed to respond to that? My impulse was to whimper and beg. Instead, I gulped down more wine, straight from the bottle. Where was the buzz that was supposed to warm me and make me feel bolder? "Then why?" I couldn't make myself ask the rest of the question.

"Because I want you so fucking badly that I'm afraid if I give in, I won't be able to stop myself from pushing that on you."

Was that hot or just scary?

I was going with *hot* because I still wanted his mouth on me as badly as I had last night. I rubbed the crystal from Nico—*please let this be what he says it is.* "Then there shouldn't be anything stopping you now."

This was dangerous. I knew as soon as I said something that I was playing with fire. And fuck it if I wasn't desperate to be scorched from the inside out.

CHAPTER 14

BRAGI

The necklace Nico gave Magnus may stop me from influencing her, but it didn't stop me from feeling her. Or him. She wanted us both and so did he.

As for me...

My restraint had been worn to a nub over the last week, and her *there shouldn't be anything stopping you* made it vanish. I strolled across the room, savoring the build of anticipation as I approached, walked around the counter, and stopped next to her.

"Do I really haunt your dreams?" Magnus was both timid and bold, like those sour sweet gummy candies she liked so much.

I didn't care that Nico watched us, lust and hesitation spilling from him, as long as he didn't stop me. I wanted to touch Magnus so badly, my body ached. To grip the back of her neck and crush my mouth to hers and tear off what little clothing she wore so I could fuck her until the way she screamed my name would make a god of fertility envious.

"Yes." I was going to savor the moment instead. She wasn't a dime-store peppermint stick. She was a delicate patisserie, meant to melt in my mouth one delicious bite at a time.

Magnus continued to rub her finger over Nico's crystal, and caught her bottom lip between her teeth.

I gripped her chin loosely and freed the fleshy swell with my thumb. The simple touch was a shock to my system and I struggled to keep my brain online amid the rush that flowed between us. "May I kiss you?"

"Yes," she whispered.

I could try to brace myself for what came next, but I refused to deprive myself of any of this experience. I traced a light touch over her skin, relishing the swell of expectation from both Magnus and Nico then dipped my head and brushed my lips over hers.

Oh, fuck me, she tasted incredible. Emotion splashed across my senses. With her barely-audible gasp, her heart fractured and mended itself, and her desire flooded me.

I pressed in harder, deepening the kiss, claiming her mouth and dancing my tongue with hers. I wanted to glut myself on this buffet, especially when she gripped my shirt tightly in her fists as if her life depended on it.

This was glorious, and there was no way I was taking her in the kitchen. When I broke away, her whimper of disappointment mingled with my groan. "Let's take this someplace more conducive to taking our time." I looked at Nico. "Are you coming with us?" I already knew the answer, but it was polite to ask.

He nodded. "Yes."

"Magnus?" I met her gaze, and almost stumbled and drown in the pools of emerald staring back at me. "Is he coming with us?"

"Yes." The mischievous smile that flitted onto her face was dangerous.

Walking upstairs would take too much time. Time I could be spending devouring Magnus. I took her hand and Nico's, and teleported us up to my room.

Their desires were enough to drown me, and it would be a blissfully happy death, but I had to be careful not to lose myself in their emotions. If I did this right, what they were feeling would wash over me, and I could let it all flow around me rather than allowing my empathy to name everything.

I let my lust blend with theirs, but I refused to mute those pieces of Magnus that had first drawn me to her—the purity of spirit. Her fierceness and loyalty. The strength and love she had for those people she felt deserved the recognition.

As it all spilled through me, I found myself drunk on her need. On Nico's. On my own.

I wanted to dine on what was in Magnus's heart until I couldn't think. I knotted my fingers in her hair and yanked lightly, eliciting a gasp, and crushed my mouth to hers to swallow her groans. Cradling her face, I kissed her until nothing else existed in my universe except her soft lips turned hard under my demand.

Nico was at her side, brushing her hair from her neck. Gliding his mouth along that luscious curve, then nibbling her skin.

Part of me wanted to hurt Magnus. Not a lot. Just enough to make her groans louder. One of the biggest struggles I had with our sessions in the clearing was when her pain and arousal bled together. Which they did a lot more often than either of us mentioned.

The light stings turned her on. The ascending slices of magic. Each time we started, she wanted a sexual release as much as I did.

And tonight we got that.

"You two keep doing what you're doing." I murmured against her mouth, then pulled away and left Nico to tease her.

I opened the trunk tucked into my closet, pulled out a silk rope and a tanto, and drank in Magnus's spike of anticipation. I returned to where she stood with Nico at the foot of the bed. The rope went around her wrists, before I attached it to the top of the four-poster bed frame. There was no slack, and her feet barely touched the floor.

"Too much?" I knew it wasn't.

Her playful smirk was everything. "Just enough."

If I got any harder, I wouldn't need the knife—I could use my cock to cut. When I drew the ancient, folded blade from its sheath, Magnus sucked in a sharp breath at the sight.

Was it possible to hear feelings drool with need?

It absolutely was.

I pressed the back of the blade to her breastbone, and glided under her bra. With a simple flick of my wrist, the sharper-than-razor steel sliced the fabric, and with a tug from Nico, the restraint fell away, exposing her breasts. Her shorts and panties were next. It took just as little effort to cut both away, though the cotton stuck to her damp skin as I pulled the ruined clothing away.

"*Creation* you're stunning." I stepped back to admire the display that was Magnus, and sample the pleased glee that she felt at my praise.

I grabbed the sheath for the tanto.

"You're not going to put that away without drawing blood." Magnus sounded offended, but she was half-teasing.

If I drew the sharp edge along her skin, I'd spend too much time looking for her limits. Tonight wasn't the night for that—she'd suffered too much recently.. Instead, I sliced along my own palm. Blood welled up, but the cut healed instantly. I wiped both blade and skin on a clean cotton rag, then put the knife away.

Tonight, I'd taste Magnus instead. Lavish her with kisses. Lick along her body and bury my face between her legs.

I took my time working my way down her torso, while Nico focused on her breasts. Dragging my tongue along her slit, lapping at her juices, was heaven.

I dove my tongue inside her and devoured her until she was teetering on the edge of orgasm, and then I pulled back. Each time I dove in again, it took a little more to push her back to that edge, and each time I eased up before she came.

When Magnus was panting and writhing and yanking against her restraints, I relented. I plunged my tongue deep into her opening, pressed my fingers to her clit, and brought her to climax.

I stayed there, delivering pleasure and thriving on the flavor, until her body was shuddering and she wobbled on her legs.

Nico pressed into her back, between her wings, holding her upright. As I reached up to undo her restraints, I kissed him hard, giving him a taste of what he'd missed and capturing Magnus between us.

Her body went limp when the ropes fell away, but she recovered enough to look me in the eye. "I want more." The pleading in her voice, in her heart, was impossible to ignore. "Please? I want to feel you both. I want *you.*"

If she said that in just the right tone, the words alone might be enough to make me come.

"I can't deny a request like that." I took one of her hands and Nico took the other. We half helped, half lifted her onto the bed, so she was on all fours in the middle of the mattress.

When we were certain she was all right like that, Nico knelt behind her. I felt both of their reactions when he penetrated her from behind, and a potent cocktail of jealousy and desire filled my veins.

He loved the way she felt, wrapped around his cock.

She was both escaping and soaring with the sensation of being filled.

And I couldn't linger in their emotion much longer. It was too dangerous.

I unzipped my slacks, freed my cock, and pressed it to Magnus's lips. She opened without hesitation and drew me in. The warm, wet sheath of her mouth, the way she traced along my shaft with her tongue, was almost enough to keep me focused on the physical.

But as Nico and I rocked her between us, fucking her while she sucked, she slipped closer to a trance-like state. That was a tempting but dangerous place to let myself linger.

Nico slipped a hand forward, to find Magnus's clit. When he teased, she jerked toward pleasure.

I sought out one of her breasts, to roll a nipple between my fingers.

The combination yanked her to orgasm again, and when she came, Nico was lost enough in her that he spilled inside her.

Their climaxes filled me. Caressed me from the inside out. Sliced away the last of my control. I fucked Magnus's face harder, until I came, barely aware of filling her mouth. Of the mess I made, as it dribbled down her chin.

The intensity in the room lingered, despite us having all slowed to a stop. It was heady and delicious. I made Magnus lay on her stomach, and cleaned her up. Then Nico and I settled into bed on either side of her.

With the cloud of pleasure fading in a pleasant haze of post-coital bliss, my mind could operate on all thrusters again. I was awash in my partners' emotions, and I wanted to hide from the world in here.

Instead, reality forced me to make sense of what they were feeling. On the one hand, it was less complicated than before. Nico didn't trust me, but he wanted to. Magnus hadn't admitted it to herself, but she wanted this, the closeness, the connection flowing between us, long term. There were still some things keeping her from being there, but not many.

None of that mattered. The instant they discovered—she discovered—I was hiding Dahlia's true fate from her, this would be over.

Was it better or worse that I'd gotten this taste before I lost her? Lost them?

I didn't know.

CHAPTER 15

BRAGI

Lying next to Magnus and Nico was…

Words escaped me, but the emotion was there, potent and mixed with theirs. I'd missed Nico so intensely, and this reminded me of what we had. It was so *real*. And Magnus…

I was obsessed with her, and I didn't care who fucking knew it.

"I need to know something," Magnus said softly. She was unsure, which was unlike her.

"Anything." Not quite the truth on my part, but close enough. She wouldn't ask the one thing I was lying about, so it didn't matter.

She was lying on her stomach between Nico and me, her wings tucked in as far as they could be, and her feet kicked up in the air, bent at the knees and crossed at the ankles. "Everyone on the TOM board is there for a reason. What's yours? What prophecy are you trying to prevent happening?"

Ah. *That* question. "That I'll lose my power."

"Mortality?" Nico said the word with a hint of fear and disgust.

"Worse. I'd still be immortal, *the god who isn't a god, who lives to see the end of eternity.*" I remembered Urd's words as if she was whispering them in my ear now.

Magnus dropped her head on to her folded arms and studied me from the prone position. "The prophecies don't always mean what you think. You know that, right? And sometimes they're just wrong."

Sometimes *Dahlia's* were wrong. And last I saw, she didn't know how to control her power. Not that I was going to risk saying her name. Besides, "This isn't something I read in one of the books. Urd told me herself. She answered my questions. She shared the vision with me." And I'd felt her pity. Her disgust.

"That's why you know how to help Magnus heal," Nico said.

No reason to hide that. "Yes. I learned in the hopes it could be used on me."

"But you came for us the first time we were fighting Vidar." It hurt Magnus to talk about this. It was the beginning of the end for her relationship with Dahlia. "He knows you're not on TOM's side anymore."

"My reasons haven't changed from the one I gave you before," I said. "I don't share their other goals and I'm no longer willing to destroy the world to accomplish mine."

Nico's *hmm* was as noncommittal as he was conflicted.

"But you weren't too clear on *why* they changed." Magnus needed an answer. She was looking for a reason to let go of the last of her hesitation about trusting me.

My answer wasn't for her friends' ears, but here, in the safety and privacy of my space, I could tell her. "Because of you."

She wasn't sure how she felt about that. Should she swoon? Be defensive?

"You don't *feel* the way anyone else does." I needed to explain this in a way she'd understand. "No one does; each set of emotion is a slightly different flavor, but yours... You're loyalty and strength and sincerity and love in a blend that's uniquely intoxicating." I wanted to wax poetic for hours, but she might see that as too much. "It made me realize that a world that could produce you, despite everything, might be worth letting survive."

Nico wanted to be skeptical, but he agreed. He knew I meant it and he knew why.

Magnus was skeptical too, but for different reasons. "I'm not that great. I'm just me. Granted,

I'm pretty fucking awesome, but I don't know that I'm all those things you said."

"Do you have a favorite flavor?" My question wasn't as random as it seemed. I would get to my point quickly.

"I don't know... Sour cherry."

I brushed her hair from her face, studying her green eyes, her freckles, her button nose... "You're mine, and I know exactly what you taste like."

Pink colored her cheeks. "Okay." She still didn't agree with me, but she believed me.

Could I keep her after all? Her pain would fade with time, and so would Nico's doubt. How long could I convince her to stay here? Him? Long enough the world and its prophecies moved on without us?

I didn't realize I'd dozed off until fear and grief jerked me awake. The feelings weren't mine—Magnus was curled into a ball against me, whimpering in her sleep.

Her wings were gone. Was that part of the nightmare or a sign of control?

I glanced up to see Nico watching her with concern as well. He met my gaze with a questioning *wake her or let her sleep*? Letting her suffer, even in her dreams, was unfathomable. With a gentle shake of her shoulder, I whispered her name, hoping to not startle her.

She sat up with a start, her gaze as unfocused as her emotions. "Dahlia?"

Fuck.

"Just us." Nico felt bad for her.

"I'm sorry." I wished the words didn't hold as much meaning as they did.

Magnus erased her grief behind a tight smile, but the feeling still hid under the surface. "*Just you* is still pretty good." She mostly meant the words.

Given that she was trying to move on from the dream, it was okay to point out, "your wings are hidden."

"I can feel them, though." She flexed her shoulder blades.

Nico stood and tugged her to her feet. They both looked incredible, standing in my bedroom wearing nothing. Magnus moved away from the bed a meter or so, and her wings blinked into sight.

Stunning.

She spread them their full width, tucked them to her back, then made them vanish again. "Are they doing what it feels like?" She spun to face my full-length mirror. She stood naked and proud, Nico's necklace stark at the base of her throat, as she admired her wings in their various postures.

It was a vision I wanted burned into my memory forever.

"It's working." Magnus's glee was potent.

Watching her, feeling her, had me hard. "It definitely is."

Nico raised an eyebrow and the look he shot me said he knew what I was thinking.

I shrugged, not caring who knew, and climbed from the bed to enjoy this moment in a more hands-on capacity. I slid up behind Magnus in front of the mirror, and she tucked her wings away without hesitation. When her gaze met mine in our reflections, our desires spiked together.

"I could watch you like this for hours. Days," I said. Heat radiated toward me, carried on lust, and I settled my hands on her stomach. If I stood here much longer, I wouldn't ever let her go.

Tempting.

Until I remembered how I nearly lost myself in her, in Nico, last night.

"You should go shower. Get ready for our next session." I kissed her shoulder.

Her pout was all for show. "Or, we could all clean up together."

I'd like that so very much. I forced myself to straighten up, and steadied her on her own feet. "By yourself, so you have some alone time before we start. I promise I have to suffer the same fate."

The three of us returned to our respective rooms to get ready for another round of healing, and I ensured I returned to the clearing by myself first, to strengthen the protective barriers.

None of the preparation mattered. When all three of us arrived, Nico was more interested in playful flirting, and while Magnus was bothered by his lack of discipline, she loved the light breather. Her heart wasn't here, anyway. She was still lingering on the memory of feeling Dahlia so close last time we were here.

CHAPTER 16

NICODEMUS

The first two times I sat in on Magnus's healing therapy, I didn't see any of the screaming and missed most of the agony I'd been warned about. I was quite grateful for that reprieve.

The third time, I wasn't so lucky. Rather, she wasn't. She did sound like she was being tortured, and the reality of watching, not being able to step in, was far worse than I imagined. I didn't feel bad for me, but I ached for her. I wanted so badly to bring a stop to things and rescue her.

Her serious warnings before we started were the only thing that kept me from interfering once she and Bragi got going.

How did Bragi do this more than once a day? How did Magnus?

When Bragi announced that they were finished,

she slumped with relief. However, her aura glowed a hint brighter. More life thrummed through her.

I let them sit and catch their breath. I knew I needed a reprieve and it technically had nothing to do with me.

When their panting had stopped and their flushes faded, I asked, "What happens next?"

Magnus glanced over her shoulder at Bragi with a look I didn't see.

His shrug in return was one I caught and understood. *It's up to you.*

Magnus looked at me. "Usually we go hide in our rooms and pretend we don't desperately want each other."

Bragi rolled his eyes and shook his head.

I let a smile slip out. To me, it was clear how many ways Bragi was holding back, and the clash with Magnus's boldness was fascinating.

"We're not doing that anymore, I assume?" I figured *no* since everyone had slept with everyone at this point.

"Doing...?" Bragi let the question hang in the air. "The wanting or the holding back?"

"*We*? Bold of you to assume anything," Magnus's voice was teasing.

I chuckled. "After the way my cock has been used recently, yes I *am* assuming."

"I didn't hear any complaints while it was happening," Magnus said.

"I'm not complaining now, either. I'm simply making an observation."

Bragi nudged Magnus to her feet, and his hand lingered on the small of her back as he stood next to her. "We shouldn't stay here, whatever it is we do." He nudged her toward the exit.

She paused and stretched her arms above her head, then rocked side to side. Every movement was graceful and stunning. "I need to work some kinks out." She caught her bottom lip between her teeth. "I didn't mean it that way. Feel free to assume I did anyway." She winked at me. "But I need some sort of physical workout. To run, to hit the bags, or something. Tell me you have a gym in this place or anything, Bragi."

He nudged us both into the house. "I have an entire back yard if you want to run."

"He also has a weight room in the basement. Though I have no idea how modern it is." It had been a few decades since I was down there.

"It's been updated," Bragi said. "And feel free to use it and abuse it."

"If you'd like a spotter..." I left the suggestion hanging.

Magnus grinned. "I'd love that, yes."

"Nico can show you where it is." Bragi turned away. "I'll catch you both in a little bit."

I was a little surprised he wasn't joining us, but I suspected after what he'd just been through, he was dealing with empathy overload. I lead Magnus further into the house, and down the stairs to the basement.

The room we stepped into was far more modern than I expected, even after Bragi's description of *updated*. Mirrors lined the walls, stainless steel free weights were on one side, a canvas body bag hung from the ceiling next to a speed bag, and half the room was lined with padded mats.

"Do you spar?" Magnus asked.

Not with her. That was the wrong answer, though I suspected she'd figure it out soon enough. "I box. As for if I do it against other people, it depends on who trained you. Hel was a scary fighter."

"Starkad was our hand-to-hand instructor."

The name sent ice running down my spine. Berserker. Wolf. Terrifyingly fierce, and loyal only to his Valkyrie. That he'd taught her made my answer easy—I'd let her assume my *no* was because of his fighting style. "No, I do not spar."

"Care to explain why not?" She was going to push the issue.

"Berserkers fight dirty—anything to win—and that one is more terrifying than most."

Magnus raised her brows. "Fair point. I was going to argue *not when you get to know him*, but yeah, he's still a scary bastard." In spite of her words, her tone was dismissive.

"They didn't teach you much respect for immortals at that school, did they?"

She nodded at the body bag. "Hold that for me?"

I stepped up to the heavy canvas, wrapped my arms halfway around it, and leaned my weight into it.

She let out a few test punches, and I used the warm up to check my resistance. Then she wrapped her fingers and pulled on lightly padded gloves. "Do you know what TOM was?" She opened with a side kick, and flowed into a series of varied punches. "I'm not being condescending. I have no idea how much the outside world is aware of what went on there."

"I know they trained soldiers to do The Board's bidding."

"They told us we were worthless, and constantly pitted us against each other." She threw a few more punches, building toward a steady rhythm. "And then they trained us to kill gods." Punch, punch, kick. Kick, punch, punch, punch. "Someone who believes they're a *worthless mortal* but is still capable of killing a god is someone who doesn't fear most gods."

I had no arguments.

For the next twenty or so minutes, I was privileged to watch her skill as she attacked the bag using a unique array of styles and techniques.

As she finished, I asked, "Were you one of their best?" She had to be.

"Why would you ask that?" Was she offended?

"Because I just watched your technique."

Magnus snorted. "Any TOM soldier can do that."

"Bragi told me you were one of Hel's Nobles."

"I was one of her bottom-of-the-barrel Nobles." The shift in her voice was clear.

"You sound disgusted by that."

She stepped away from the bag enough to look me in the eye. "I am. With myself for not being good enough. With Hel for thinking I wasn't good enough..."

"You're good enough for me." That was under-whelming.

The clench of her jaw implied she agreed. "Do you want a turn? Because it's creepy if you just came down here to watch me work out."

I'd come down with the offer of company and spotting her, but it had been a while since I'd landed my fists on something solid, and it might feel good. There was no need to wrap my knuckles or wear gloves—I healed instantly, and the pain was just as fleeting.

My technique, if it could be called that, was nothing like Magnus's. Where hers was grace and years of training, mine was brute force. The conver-sation faded to nothing as I lit into the bag with hooks and crosses and jabs.

When I finished, I found Magnus watching me

with wide eyes. "Holy shit," she said. "Were you a boxer?"

"I have boxed. Professionally." I was also pleased she noticed.

"But you don't want to spar with me."

I was going to have to tell her the truth eventually. "If we fight, I'll hold back, and you'll get mad and kick my ass."

"If you know that will be the outcome, why hold back in the first place?"

"I can't stand the thought of hitting you."

She twisted her mouth and crossed her arms. "After that entire conversation about how I was trained, you're going to be the patronizing asshole who can't hit a woman?"

"I'm going to be the *smitten* asshole who can't hit *you.*"

An ice barrier might as well have formed around Magnus, for the chill she gave off. "That's swell. I need a shower. Alone. Ciao, Mr. Smitten Asshole."

I'd love to think I should get points for honesty, but I doubted she saw things that way. When I looked at Magnus, I still saw the vision from my dreams. The auburn-haired Valkyrie who owned my heart and soul. However, getting to know her, I saw the real person underneath. The three-dimensional individual who may not belong on a pedestal, but was far better than she had been in my dreams.

The rest of the night passed without my running

into either Magnus or Bragi. Was he smug that I'd made her angry?

I wasn't kicked out of her session the next day, but she didn't acknowledge me either. She looked past me at every opportunity, and her screams cut me to the quick regardless.

As we walked away from the clearing, she stayed about a meter in front of me, providing a stunning view, and Bragi fell into step beside me.

"What did you do to piss her off?" he asked.

"I refused to fight her."

He snorted. "You're an idiot."

"You would have acted differently in my place?" I didn't believe that for an instant.

"You'll notice I didn't put myself in your place. There's no sin if I never have to make the decision. You should be familiar with that."

I winced at the indirect reference to my long-term neutrality.

"I'm right here," Magnus called over her shoulder as we stepped into the house. "I can hear everything the two of you are saying."

"Your point is?" Was Bragi trying to provoke her?

She spun and looked at us. Finally. "Which books in the library did you write?"

Odd change of subject.

We stopped in the doorway to the room in question.

"Do you want a list?" Bragi asked.

"I want to know where they're located."

Fascinating. Where was she going with this?

"You act like I keep them all grouped together," Bragi said.

He did.

Magnus nodded. "I'm guessing they're on one of the shelves along the wall. You want everyone to know which collection is yours the instant they walk in the room, even if you never say a word about it."

"She's got your number, mate." I was entertained by this exchange.

Bragi let out a heavy sigh. "The shelf behind the desk."

The very first one anybody saw upon walking into the room, no matter which angle they approached from.

"Called it." Magnus walked to the shelf farthest from that one, plucked a thin book from a shelf at her eye level, and walked out again. "I'll be in my room," she said as she passed us.

I watched her ass sway as she headed down the hallway and out of sight, both entertained and frustrated with the day's conclusion.

"I'd ask if you want a translation of how she feels, but you've already figured it out," Bragi said.

I shook my head. "I see why you're infatuated."

"You've only seen a hint of what captivates me, and it only gets more frustrating."

"Aren't you supposed to tell me it gets better?"

"Nope." Bragi popped the *p*. "Not with her. Not with you. Infuriating fucking redheads."

I grinned at the affection in his curse. "I missed you too."

"I know." He gripped the back of my neck and gave me a long kiss that I felt all the way in the past. "It's good to have you back in the house. In my life."

During the next few therapy sessions, Magnus remained cool and aloof. It wasn't as unbearable as her screams, but I still didn't care for it.

As we wrapped up one afternoon, she hopped to her feet. "I really need to hit the bag again. Are you willing to admit you were wrong, Nico?"

"I'm not wrong."

"You refuse to hit me because I'm a girl."

That wasn't true. I'd fought any number of goddesses across my lifetimes. "I refuse to hit you because I care about you. I wouldn't do it to Bragi, either."

She huffed and headed toward the basement. I followed, Bragi stayed behind.

Magnus faced me when we reached the workout room. "I'm giving you permission."

"Is this the only way to get you to talk to me like a normal person again?" I didn't appreciate being backed into this corner.

"No. But it's the fastest way."

"Tell me why it matters... Besides the fact that you think I'm a chauvinist prick. Because I promise you, it's not about your gender." I had to know.

She looked at the ceiling for a moment before she met my gaze again. "I've spent most of my life listening to immortals tell me I'm not good enough, strong enough, or *enough* enough, but they still demanded too much from me. It's hard for me to trust anyone who refuses to admit what I'm capable of."

"This was never about what you could do," I said. "But on the mats. I'll do this. What are the rules?"

Her smile was almost worth the concession by itself. "Only two rules—it's not over until you tap out or pass out, and no tapping out just to end things early."

"Agreed."

We faced off on the mats, and she was all energy, bouncing on the balls of her toes. Since she had the high-end moves and I only had my fists, I let her throw the opening volley.

She was fast, darting in to probe my defenses from different angles. I blocked each weak punch and kick, but didn't throw any of my own.

She landed a foot to the back of my knee that sent me stumbling, and I recovered quickly. I wasn't the only one holding back. Her next flurry of attacks required me to retaliate, or it would be clear I wasn't trying, but I couldn't bring myself to put any force into the punches.

Magnus's growl was as fierce and infuriated as any berserker's. "Rule number three—this is bullshit. I'm done."

"You can't change the rules mid-fight." I grabbed her wrist as she tried to stalk away.

She spun in a flash, diving into me, catching me off-balance, and throwing me to my back on the mat. I gasped at the impact, more out of shock than pain. "You can't promise to not hold back, and then hold back." She straddled me and pinned my arms above my head. "You promised."

I had, and it was impossible to ignore her hurt. I didn't want to disappoint Magnus or lie to her, and with her latest move, the weight of her body on mine, and her heat, adrenaline spilled through me. Letting a little bit of leash out on my restraint, I rolled us both, intending to pin her instead.

She used the change in leverage to kick me back, and bounced to her feet.

I was up in an instant too, frustrated I hadn't seen her move coming, and ready to strike.

"See? I knew you could do it," Magnus taunted.

Fine. We'd do things her way. I swung and she ducked, but I was ready with a follow-up punch, which connected. I didn't have time to worry about if I'd hurt her, as she swept a leg and knocked my feet out from under me. She jumped, aiming an attack on her way down.

I rolled to the side, all in on this match. I had to lean into instinct to keep up, which meant no more focusing on pulling my punches. Not that it mattered, when I did connect, Magnus barely flinched, and she gave as good as she got.

Until I managed to pin her to the mat. She didn't struggle as she lay underneath me, eyes wide, with her smelling like sweat and desire and licking her lips.

That pause was enough for my brain to catch up. For me to feel every inch of where our bodies met, and for my own want to rush back in. The only thing stopping me from leaning in and kissing her was that she hadn't tapped out.

Still, when she tilted her head up and brushed her lips over mine, I wanted to press the rest of my body to hers and fuck her right here.

Letting my guard down was a mistake. She rolled us both, and landed on top of me, with her knee between my legs and pressed uncomfortably against my now-hard cock.

I was done. I tapped the mat.

"Remember the rules." Magnus didn't move.

"I remember what it's like to be kneed in the balls, and even if it heals right away, that's one of those pains that lingers."

She laughed lightly, hopped to her feet, and offered me a hand up.

As I stood, I wrapped an arm around her waist and kissed her hard.

Her laugh hummed against my lips. She nudged me away playfully. "Can we keep doing this going forward? No more of this holding back bullshit?"

"I look forward to it." More than I had most things in a long time.

I walked Magnus upstairs. "I'm getting a drink, if you want something," I said.

"Sure." She followed me into the kitchen.

Bragi was already there, and had two glasses of apple juice with sliced strawberries waiting for us. I recognized the drink the instant I saw it, because I used to make the same thing when he and I were together.

Magnus's smile grew and she grabbed one of the drinks. "Just like at TOM."

"Just like," Bragi said.

Was I jealous he'd shared our drink with someone else, or pleased he remembered that moment enough to pass it along?

Magnus took a long swallow before setting her glass down. "I forgot how much I missed this."

"Same," I said, looking at Bragi.

He didn't seem bothered by my scrutiny.

"Do you plan on joining us downstairs at any point?" Magnus sipped her drink.

"Not the way you're asking," Bragi said.

She cocked her head to one side. "Why not?"

"Because the way you two are riding that line between will we or won't we, I'd be fucking a hole in the mat before I got a chance to participate in the real activities."

It was certainly an interesting visual. I probably shouldn't take Bragi so literally.

Magnus leaned in, elbows on the counter, pressing her breasts together. "You could fuck a hole in me."

Bragi seemed to consider this for a moment. "Tempting, but giving you new holes is counterproductive to the healing we've been doing."

"Hmm..." Magnus pursed her lips, looking absolutely kissable. "Nico would volunteer, if you'd rather I just watch."

I was going to argue at being dragged into this conversation but, "She's right, I would."

"I know. But if *I* want sex"— Bragi used his full body to pin me to the wall—"I'm not going to fuck around with wresting first. I'm going straight for the fucking." He dropped his hand to stroke my cock through my sweats, and crushed his mouth to mine.

Magnus's grunt of delight mingled with mine and fueled the flames threatening to erupt between Bragi and me.

A guy could get used to spending his time like this.

CHAPTER 17

MAGNUS

Bragi confounded me, with the pressing in hot and heavy then pulling away so quickly it gave me whiplash.

There was very little mysterious about Nico. Even when he held back, it was never for long.

Was it fucked up that I didn't know which I preferred?

Fortunately, the more time I spent with them, the less likely it seemed I would have to choose. The three of us didn't make it to bed together the night we discussed fucking holes in things, much to my dismay, but we wound up in naked, orgasmic bliss, the next night.

As the days passed, the therapy sessions would have bled together if it weren't for the fun of rolling around on the mats with Nico, and both of us falling into bed with Bragi.

Nico and I were in the basement again, sparring. I planned on making this session and anything that came after, last as long as possible, thanks to me not wanting to return to nightmares about losing Dahlia.

"How does your reincarnation work?" I launched a spinning kick at him and connected with more force than I expected.

Nico stumbled before finding his balance. "I apologize. I wasn't expecting that question."

"Was that a bad thing to ask?" Apparently I'd just stumbled on a weird random social faux pas.

"You're asking someone *how do you come back to life*? It's a bit personal." Nico was back to watching me circle him. "However, I suppose we've gotten quite a bit more personal recently."

"I'd say so." I was a little hurt he'd hesitated. Did I think we were that close? We weren't always and forever, but I could see us getting there. I'd shared bits of myself no one else knew about but Dahlia—of my thoughts and likes and dislikes and more—with both Nico and Bragi.

Nico tossed out a jab that was more about testing my defenses than connecting, and I stepped out of his reach without pause. His smile was easy. "I'd say so too. It doesn't work the same for me as for a lot of the others, like Kirby. I come back as me, not a baby or another person. I'm me, in a body pretty much like the one I have now, and I always wake up at home. As if I'd just taken a long nap."

"Where's home?" I darted in with a feint that he didn't fall for, and I jumped back before his counter could connect with me.

"A little village in Wales, near the ocean. I'll show you on a map later, because if I tell you how to pronounce it, it won't mean anything to you."

That was true. I was fluent in seven different languages—every Noble knew at least five—including Russian, but I'd never gotten the hang of Welsh. Not even with lessons from Gwydion. "Looking forward to it."

Bragi walked up to the doorway, but didn't step into the room. I pretended not to notice, and I saw my opening in Nico's defenses. I committed to a fake-out that would take me off-balance if Nico didn't fall for it.

He did, and with a sweep of my legs, I had him on his back, and I straddled him.

Pretty much my favorite way to end any of these matches, no matter who ended up on top. What now? Should I put on a show for Bragi? Continue to pretend I didn't know he was there, and tap out despite being on top, so I could make out with Nico?

So many options.

Given this was the first time I'd ever seen Bragi down here, I wanted to know why. "I got the impression you never joined us, because you didn't want to deal with us hitting each other." I glanced over my shoulder at him.

He strode into the room. "I feel regardless, no matter where I am, and the thing about spending centuries immersing myself in others emotions is if I hadn't developed a little bit of a sadistic streak, it would've driven me mad." He paused at the edge of the mat, studying us. "Besides, despite fucking every other night, the sexual tension and denial between the two of you is so thick that I'm walking around with a perpetual hardon. I figured it was time for me to at least enjoy the view."

Which had to be fantastic. I shifted my weight against Nico enough to rest just below his waist, and I felt him harden in an instant. "Do you like what you see?" I asked.

"Frequently." Bragi left his shoes at the edge of the mat, approached, and tugged me to my feet. He offered Nico a hand up as well.

"Did you want to join us?" Nico asked as he stood.

"Oh no. Definitely not." Bragi looked me over in a way that stole my breath. "Do want to hurt you though. Just enough."

The threat delivered on a seductive tone made my heart hammer against my ribs. "You think you get one without the other?"

Bragi pressed a hand to my throat and squeezed

lightly. Enough to make my pulse roar in my ears. "I think I'll do whatever you beg me to, when it comes down to it."

"Beg you?" I had to force the words and light scoff out. I was captivated by his touch. By the way Nico pressed into my back, trapping me between them. But there was a hint of hesitation inside. Just a whisper.

Bragi glanced down at the necklace from Nico—the crystal that still hung around my neck—and his touch dropped away. "See you in our next session."

The tension in the room didn't shatter so much as it shifted from incredible to suffocating, as Bragi left.

"You die a little inside when he does that, don't you?" Nico's question jarred me.

"When he does what?"

"Those rare moments when he lets you in completely, and you feel like you've accomplished something."

Yup. Nico was thinking the same thing I was. "And then he puts the walls back up, and the face-plant gives you whiplash."

"So you turn back to me for the distraction," Nico said.

That made me sound horrible. "No. I mean, yes, but..." But what? I was going to justify my actions somehow?

Nico snorted a laugh. "That isn't reassuring."

"Bragi is so hard to read." I wasn't trying to excuse my behavior, but I did feel like I had to explain. "He opens up, he closes off, and sometimes there's no rhyme or reason to it. But you're you. I don't have to guess with you."

"No, you don't."

"And that's what I want from you—to be you. I adore you as *you*," I said. "And I want him for him. Two different desires."

Nico wove his fingers into mine. "I understand that better than you may believe. Will you join me in the library?"

That was an abrupt segue. "I suppose?"

"I won't keep you for long if you don't want." He led me upstairs, into the library, and up to the shelf I'd pulled a book from a few days ago, when I was trying to spite Bragi. "This is the next book by the author whose book you selected."

Nico had to know that I'd just picked one. It had turned out to be a poetry book, and while it was lovely and sweet, I was more of an explosions and battles kind of girl. "A favorite of yours?" I asked.

"When it comes to seducing you, yes."

"You should maybe know poetry isn't the way to my heart."

He led me back to the loveseat and pulled me to sit next to him. "Give me a few stanzas, and get up and walk out if it's not doing anything for you."

Now I was intrigued. "I'm listening." And fully prepared for flowery, Shakespearean-style sonnets.

Instead, what Nico launched into was an epic tale of rivalry turned love, that included a challenge to a duel, and sword-fighting at dawn. He knew this story, too. He glanced at the book occasionally, but for the most part he watched me, hitting all the right places for emphasis, for tension, and for all of it.

It was breathtaking, and when he finished, he closed the book and set it on my lap. "Better than a Marvel movie?" he asked.

"Don't push your luck." I stroked my thumb along the spine of the tiny tome. "But it was pretty seductive. And a girl likes to be wooed, even if she *has* already given up the pussy."

Nico laughed and shook his head. "You're a true poet yourself."

I stood, bent at the waist, and pressed my lips to his cheek in the most chaste kiss I could muster while giving him a perfect view down the front of my sports bra. "I'm going to shower and nap. Thank you for the poetry."

Though I left him behind as I headed to my room, I couldn't hide my smile at the gesture. He'd gone out of his way to pick a poem, to put on a performance, he knew I'd love. It was sexy and it was adorable.

After I washed away the sweat, I collapsed in bed. Exhaustion tended to sink in quickly when I pulled myself away from the various stimuli in the house. As I lay under the covers, a familiar sensation whispered over me. Friendly. Warm.

"Dahlia?" I muttered to the empty air.

It couldn't be. It wasn't. I drifted off and woke up in a cold sweat. I had no idea how long I'd been asleep since there were no clocks in here, but it felt like an eternity. I was still so exhausted, though. I drifted off again, and the dreams raced back. Reliving Dahlia's death. Over and over. Until I was gasping for breath when I woke up.

I was sitting in bed, knees hugged to my chest, trying and failing to will the memories into the back of my mind again. My bedroom door opened and Bragi strode in.

He climbed into bed next to me without a word, and pulled me down with my back to him. "I've got you." His voice was soft as he cradled me.

I hated this so much. The memories. The loss. Missing her.

"I wish I could take this from you," he said quietly.

"No." I appreciated the offer, but I would never ask him to do that. "Thank you, but I never want to surrender how I feel about the people I love, even when it hurts."

Bragi kissed the top of my head. "Go back to sleep. I'm here."

And he was still there when I woke up. I felt like

shit after several hours of nightmares, but I was grateful for his comfort.

"Are you up for sessions today?" Bragi asked.

There was no way I was sitting alone with my thoughts, or letting this impotence of mine go on for longer than it needed to. "Yes. Unless I'm on my death bed again, I'm up for this."

He extracted himself from me and brushed his lips over my cheek. "I'll meet you there."

The sunlight streaming through my window didn't erase the shadows from my mind, but I dressed anyway. I headed to the doorway to find Bragi waiting. Nico was already inside when we stepped into the other realm. He was sitting on a picnic blanket with an honest-to-god wicker basket next to him.

"For when you're done," Nico patted the basket.

They must both be in on this, and the sweet gesture made me smile.

I suffered through the pain and swallowed most of my screams. This was worth it. This was how I got my vengeance, and any agony was worth slaughtering the gods who played a part in Dahlia's death.

Instead of leaving when we were done, Bragi and I joined Nico on the blanket. The two of them laid out lunch, and kept up a thread of conversation that didn't require me to participate. The sunshine and the company helped my mood as much as putting some distance between myself and sleep.

"Will I ruin the moment if I ask how the two of you met?" I wanted to keep hearing about them. Anything to not think about my own past.

Nico shook his head. "However, you will ruin the mood if you ask why we broke up."

"Which Nico has more or less already told you," Bragi said.

I wrinkled my nose at the thought of talking about sadness. No thank you. "I want the falling in love story, not the falling apart story."

"Why?" Bragi studied me.

I stared back, willing him to read my thoughts as well as my feelings. "Why not?"

"That's not an answer."

If he was going to be infuriating, I wasn't interested. "You gave me a not-answer first. If you don't want to tell me, say that you don't want to tell me."

"Vienna. 1781." Nico to the rescue.

"The opera," Bragi added.

Nico looked at him, a wistful look in his eyes. "Mozart. You were fucking him."

Bragi smiled in a warm way I rarely saw. "And you stole me away."

"The two of you would never have lasted anyway," Nico said.

I liked this story. It was simple. It was sweet.

"Because he died young?" Bragi asked.

Maybe that part wasn't sweet.

Nico chuckled. "Because your egos didn't fit in the same room."

I laughed. Seeing the two of them like this, teasing each other, was perfect.

"Well?" Bragi looked at me again.

I wasn't sure why. "Well what? It's a lovely story."

"You're not going to scoff in disbelief and say *I can't believe you fucked Mozart*?"

I most certainly was not. Of all the stories I'd heard from the two of them, of all the creatures they'd told me existed, and all the tales Bragi and Nico had spun, this one was the most plausible. "You already know I believe you. Though I am sad I never got to witness it."

"You get to see *us* together, and that's much better than Mozart and me." Bragi leaned into Nico and nuzzled his neck—*that* caught me off-guard. But it was a fantastic sight.

"It really is, now that you mention it." I'd watch it all day. Though I'd prefer to be a part of it.

"You don't strike me as a waiting on the sidelines kind of girl." Nico was the one to read my mind this time.

"I'm not. Watching is fun for a few minutes, but put me in the game sooner rather than later."

Bragi moved closer to me, wrapped his arm around my waist, and pulled me into him. He bit playfully along my neck. "Consider yourself in."

Nico knelt in front of me and brushed his lips over mine, drawing a sigh of delight from me. He leaned past me to kiss Bragi, but returned to me quickly. Between the attention from the two of them, I couldn't help but laugh with delight.

A tiny thought pierced the back of my mind. I hoped that Dahlia would forgive me for having a little fun, so soon after...

CHAPTER 18
BRAGI

With each healing session, Magnus gained access to a little more of her magic, but the milestones were the real mood lifters—when she could summon her Valkyrie armor again, and it was gleaming and new. When she could access her weapons. Her magical shield...

I immersed myself in all of their emotions. Magnus's glee and pain. Nico's desire and regret. Anything they felt was another morsel for me to devour, and the thing I gorged myself on the most was their adoration as they fell for each other, and me.

We were in the clearing again, suffering through another round of Magnus's agony, when I felt something slip inside her, and click into place.

She gasped and sat straight up, and a soft glow

encompassed her. It was like placing the last piece into a puzzle, and it was glorious.

"You're done," I said.

Her elation was a sweet nectar as she hopped to her feet. "Seriously? Are you serious?"

"Frequently."

"*Ahh.*" She squealed with excitement and threw her arms around my neck. "Thank you. Thank you, *thank you.*"

I pulled back enough to brush my lips over hers. "Any time. Always and forever for you." I murmured against her skin before deepening the kiss.

Magnus leaned into me with a contented sigh, happy for me to own her in that moment.

But the instant we broke apart, she was back to dancing and clapping. Nico swept her into his arms when she hugged him, and he gave her a long kiss as well.

Something new flitted into Magnus's mood, mingling with joy rather than pushing it out. I couldn't identify the new flavor, but it made my skin crawl and soured my mood.

"We need to make a plan." The instant she said the words, my gut sank. "I have to call Kirby. Frey. Beg his forgiveness. You have to help us find the rest of the board." She focused on me.

Absolutely, one-hundred-percent out of the question. Not that I was going to phrase it that way to her. "You need to make sure you're really ready."

"I've been ready for weeks, and now my Valkyrie magic is too." Magnus bounced on the balls of her feet. She stopped abruptly and sadness washed over her. "I can finally say *goodbye* to Dahlia."

If I offered some concessions, could I keep her from other things a while longer? Or was this about to snowball into me losing her?

Whatever I needed to do, I wasn't ready for Magnus to be gone from my life. "Go change while Nico and I make lunch, and we can talk about what kind of a memorial is appropriate for Dahlia." The words nearly stuck in my throat. They weren't a lie, but they hid an enormous deception.

Nico and I didn't say much as we worked in the kitchen. He was feeling a similar sort of pending loss to mine, though his wasn't as intense—he didn't expect Magnus to completely vanish. We prepped a board with cold cuts, cheese, and meat. Magnus would be too distracted to do more than nibble.

When she joined us, she was wearing more normal clothing for her, and I instantly missed the short shorts and sports bras. She sat, but she didn't sit still.

"Okay, so I've been thinking." She nibbled as she talked. "If we launch any sort of brute force attack on one god, the rest may assume we're coming for them, so we need to do this stealthily. Fortunately, Frey is the perfect ally for that. And Kirby and Brit—

Oh, those bullets, the ones that kill immortals. Can you get me some of those?"

I shook my head. "Those are under"— *Vidar's control*—"I don't know. I'll work on finding out who's assumed control of that asset." That might buy me some time, but only if she decided those were a necessity for whatever plans she made.

"Are you going to take time to mourn?" At Nico's comment, I bit back a growl. "You mentioned a memorial."

Magnus stalled, and her hands dropped limply to her sides. Her grief poured out in suffocating waves. "I don't want to do much. A simple farewell."

That I could help with. "What do you need?"

"There's a small grove of trees in Japan. Mount Yoshino. We used to promise each other, back when we were mortal, that if anything happened to us, that would be the final resting place for our ashes." Magnus's emotion around the memory was bitter-sweet and cloying. "I'd like to go there."

Out in the open. In the human world. With a very not-dead Dahlia who had the ability to feel anyone, anywhere. I was going to need every barrier I could summon to keep us divided from reality, but I'd do it for Magnus. "Okay. When do you want to go?"

"Now." She took Nico's hand and mine. "Please?"

I couldn't refuse her. "All right." I summoned the wards before I teleported us, and we arrived in Japan in an invisible bubble. It wouldn't keep people out, but it would make us a blank spot on any magical radar.

The instant the real world blinked into view, Magnus's mood shifted. It swung further into grief, and then confusion blinked in.

I followed her gaze to a tree—one, indistinct cherry tree in a wash of hundreds. The ground around it looked disturbed, as if someone had dug in the dirt at some point in the last few weeks.

This was about to be bad. I didn't know why, but the sense of foreboding that filled me was overwhelming.

Magnus stepped deliberately toward the tree, and knelt next to the loose ground. She dug, slowly at first, and then with more vigor, until she reached something I couldn't see. "What is this?" She was talking more to herself than us.

She withdrew a long ring—the kind meant to sheath an entire finger—and it ended in a terrifying looking claw.

My gut sank. Despite having been buried, the ring was clean, and it looked nearly identical to one Magnus had owned in the past. One that Dahlia gave her, that Vidar imbued with fae blood, to make it magical.

But unlike the one she'd owned before, this one was pure dragon.

She looked between it and us. "Why is this here?"

There was no reason I should know the answer, except that I did. Dahlia had beaten her to the memorial and left one of her own.

Not that I could give that as an answer. I also didn't want to lie. I braced myself for an abrupt end to the last month together.

CHAPTER 19
MAGNUS

This was all wrong, and I couldn't pinpoint why. Bragi's behavior was off. Not in an obvious way, but little twitches, pauses in his thoughts, made me question what he was hiding. He hadn't made me feel like that for weeks.

And now I was holding something in my hand that shouldn't exist. A replica of a gift that Dahlia gave me a few years ago. Artura, one of the dragons responsible for the prophecies, had destroyed it. She called it an abomination because it was made from her claw, but corrupted with a magic that wasn't meant to be wielded the way I was.

This ring didn't feel bad though. In fact, it was warmth and love and comfort, and as I held it, I swore Dahlia was standing right next to me.

Nothing mattered but finding answers. The impulse was so strong it was pushing me to act without thinking. I wasn't a big fan of following my instincts unless I knew why, but I had to. "I need to go back to my apartment."

"It doesn't exist," Bragi said. "I'm reaching for it, and it's not there."

I slid the ring on, and it fit like it was made for me. "It does exist, I can feel it." I could feel so much. The magic I'd wielded before, when I wore the old ring, was back. It gave me access to minor dragon and fae magic. The ability to put up a wall that separated worlds. The ability to penetrate someone else's, and to teleport.

I couldn't wait for Bragi to come up with an excuse. My mind was screaming *go. Now.* Taking both Nico and Bragi's hands, I brought us back to the apartment I'd shared with Dahlia. Which was in another realm rather than on earth. That was odd.

But it was also something Frey could do. Maybe it was his way of preserving Dahlia's memory. Nothing looked out of place. It was the same as the last time I'd been here, aside from not existing on the same plane I expected it to be in.

I wanted to linger in Dahlia's room. To curl up on her bed, hug her stuffed toys, and bawl.

I also wanted to know why this itch was under my skin. A feeling I couldn't reach. Couldn't scratch.

Grabbing some of my clothes, I shoved them into a bag. My phone sat on my nightstand.

That wasn't right. I'd had it at NEON, the night

before everything fell apart. I left it behind when I went to fight, because I wasn't an idiotic movie character who let their ringing phone interrupt them on a mission.

Had Frey brought that here, too? And put it in the same spot that I left it when I slept?

I looked at Nico, who was watching me with concern. And Bragi, who wore an oddly blank expression.

When I woke up the phone, dozens of voice messages were waiting for me, with timestamps in the last month. All of them from Dahlia's phone.

What the actual fuck? I was almost terrified to press *Play*. What did voices from beyond the grave say?

"Are you all right?" Nico's question made me jump.

I shook my head. "No. This is all so very wrong."

"What is?" he asked.

I looked at Bragi, and the clench of his jaw was subtle, but screamed *warning* in my head.

I played the first message.

"I miss you so much." Dahlia's voice filtered out from the phone and gripped my heart, squeezing until I nearly collapsed from the pain. "I don't know what I'm going to do without you, Magnus."

"Magnus?" Dahlia's confused voice came from behind me.

I whirled to find her standing there with Fen,

both of them looking very much alive. My world dropped out from underneath me, and I nearly fell, despite not moving. Was this another of those fucking dreams? A delusion being brought on by too much reality?

Would I wake up at any minute, sitting in Bragi's bed, sobbing?

The scene wasn't changing. Alive-Dahlia stared at me with an expression that matched my own, and took a step closer at the same time I did, her arm extended the same way mine was.

The instant our hands meet, in some sort of surreal ET, Wonder Twins moment, my heart started beating again. Hammering in my chest and in my ears.

"It's really you," she said softly.

"Oh my God, you're alive." I grabbed her wrist and pulled her into the tightest hug ever, not daring to let go. "Holy fuck. I saw you die. I thought... Oh my God." And I was crying again. Tears of happiness. Relief.

She was doing the same. Soaking the shoulder of my shirt and holding onto me like she was terrified I wasn't real.

I knew the feeling.

When we broke apart, we were both talking at once, half over each other, half finishing each other's thoughts.

"I saw you die. It was horrible."

"So I killed Vidar."

"I was so sad."

"What was I supposed to do?"

"I was broken, or I would've looked for you sooner," I said.

Dahlia glanced between me and the men I was with. "Who's he? Why are you with Bragi?"

"I didn't know where else to go. I saw you both obliterated..." My gaze landed on Fen, and my brain inched past shock. "You're alive too."

"Don't sound so surprised," Fen teased. "I'm not that easy to destroy."

But... The gears in my mind turned. It was painful. I didn't want them to. Whatever thought they were working on was about to hurt. "Does Frey know?"

"Of course." Dahlia's laugh was light. So her. "Why didn't you go to him if you thought... He'd never turn you away."

"I was so sad. So guilty." I still felt all of those feelings as if they'd only happened yesterday. "I thought he might kill me for losing both of you, and I didn't have the strength to fight... Especially not him."

Dahlia squeezed my fingers. "He'd never turn you out, I promise."

This was chaos. Giddiness and relief mingled with the memory of sorrow. Bragi must be feeling—

I turned to him, and he frowned.

"You told me you'd talked to Frey," I said. "That you made sure he knew they were gone." My thoughts and feelings were sorting themselves, and I didn't like what they were turning into.

Fen growled.

Dahlia stepped up next to me. "If he'd done that, we'd have had this reunion ages ago."

I kept my attention on Bragi, watching every twitch, and waiting to see what kind of bullshit would come out of his mouth.

I'd spent weeks grieving. Mourning. And hating myself for falling in love.

And he felt it all and held back the one piece of information that could fix everything. If I'd been in his shoes...

"You knew," I said, when he didn't speak.

"I did."

Like that, every bit of trust and affection I had for him shattered. "How long?"

"The day you woke up."

Why was I asking him anything? He was obviously capable of telling some severe lies to get what he wanted. Was there any point in asking why? "Do you even have the decency to regret it now that I know the truth?"

"I did it to protect you. I'd do it again."

No. Now that I saw reality, the lies were so clear. "You did it to keep me. Why does it matter if you can force your emotions on me, when you can trick me into loving you instead?"

Dahlia squeezed my hand, and the reassurance bolstered me.

"I'll explain if you let me," Bragi said.

Oh, I had to hear this. I gripped the crystal that hung around my neck. The gift from Nico that I'd almost taken off this morning when I changed into street clothes. "I'm listening." The best part was, Bragi would know I wasn't fully. He'd feel how deep this distrust ran.

And I hoped it fucking hurt.

He nodded. "The day you woke up, after your injuries, I got a call from Vidar—"

Fen's growl filled the room, threatening enough to terrify me, and I knew he was on my side.

"Vidar's dead. I saw him die," Dahlia said.

So did I. I saw myself kill him. But I'd also watched her die, so...

"Because your sight is to believed when it comes to any aspect of that fight?" Bragi asked. He looked at me again. "He promised me that if I kept you with me, if I kept you away from him, he wouldn't hunt you. You were hurt. You couldn't access your Valkyrie powers--"

"I remember, thanks." I cut him off.

He raised an eyebrow. "I did it to keep you safe."

"From what?" I asked. "Vague threats from

Vidar? I don't give a fuck who he goes after unless…"
And now I saw the rest of the picture.

"Magnus, please." Bragi's mask slipped, and his hard expression gave way to soft pleading. "This was always about you."

For him, maybe. I believed that, even still. But for Vidar… There were very few people I would stand in front of a god for, and half of them were in this room. Vidar swore vengeance on Fen ages ago, for killing Odin. The only reason to keep me out of the picture… "You hid me, you lied to me, so Vidar could hunt Fen?"

"Magnus—"

"And probably Dahlia in the process?" I was almost shouting in disbelief. I wanted Bragi to deny it. If he said *no, that's not it*, I might believe him. Maybe. "Is that why you did it?"

Bragi frowned. "I did it—"

"Is what I said true?" I pushed.

He pursed his lips. "I would move mountains for you."

"But you couldn't tell me the truth."

"I destroyed my standing with the members of the board, for you."

"I never asked you for that."

"I would surrender so very much, to keep you by my side."

"You barely know me."

"I love you, Magnus."

No. There was no fucking way. He didn't just—

Fen's growl increased in volume, and Dahlia tensed, ready for a fight.

Nico's scowl was etched so deeply, his face looked carved from stone.

I shook my head. "Fuck you," I said to Bragi. "You obsessive, fucking fuck. You don't love me, you want to possess me."

"I—"

"Stop." I stopped short of stomping my foot. "Don't open your mouth. Don't even think my name. Get the fuck out of my life, and pray I never see you again."

"Ma—"

"Get. The fuck. *Out.*" I screamed so loudly it left my ears ringing, and summoned the magic from the ring to force him from the room, and make sure he couldn't find us again.

This didn't ache as badly as losing Dahlia, but Bragi's betrayal hurt a hell of a lot more than his healing therapy had.

CHAPTER 20

NICODEMUS

Magnus's fury was palpable. Hell, the gods on the moon probably heard her exorcize Bragi, and I didn't blame her.

When she turned apologetic green eyes on me, my heart cracked. I was addicted to this woman.

"And you thought the screaming in the grove was bad." Her joke was weak.

"Screaming? What screaming? Who's the pretty man?" Dahlia asked.

I could already see why the two liked each other.

"Hey, now." The man with Dahlia was terrifying, but at least he'd stopped growling.

She kissed him on the cheek. "Don't worry. You're still my scary, big-bad wolf."

This wasn't... Fenrir? I'd heard dozens of stories over the years, and none of them prepared me for this. Who were these women that they tamed even the most ferocious gods?

I already knew the answer in Magnus's case. Not that I knew everything, but I'd seen enough to have a good idea.

"Now that the drama's over, how about introductions?" Magnus's voice was still tight. "Nico, this is Dahlia and Fenrir, who are apparently very much alive." *There* was a hint of giddiness. Good. "Dahlia, Fen, this is Nicodemus. His tears saved my life."

I shook their hands. "I've heard a lot about both of you."

"You don't know each other?" Dahlia looked between Fen and me. "I assumed—"

"Everyone from Chicago knew everyone else from Chicago?" Magnus asked.

Dahlia shrugged. "Well, yes, but no. There aren't as many immortals as there are people in Chicago."

"There are more than you realize, and we don't all live in the same city." Though I was about to put myself wherever they took Magnus.

Dahlia didn't look fazed. "Well, whatever." She suddenly threw her arms around my neck, nearly knocking me backwards in surprise, and gave me a tight hug. "Thank you for bringing Magnus back to us."

I squeezed back. "I don't think anything could keep you apart. You must be an incredible creature to mean so much to someone like Magnus."

Dahlia stepped back with a blush.

"She is." Fen's hand on the small of her back was subtle, but overwhelmingly possessive.

"She's the absolute best," Magnus said.

I couldn't interrupt this reunion. "I'm going to let you all catch up. Magnus, are you staying here?"

"She's staying with us." The *no arguments* was implied in Fen's tone.

Though I'd never met him, I knew he and his long-time partner owned a burlesque club in Chicago underground. I'd known even before Magnus told me. I gently tugged Magnus to me, tracing my thumb along the back of her knuckles.

Her friends' eyebrows shot toward the ceiling.

"I'll find you when I know where I'm staying." I held her hand and her gaze. "If you want me to. I'm not him, I didn't know what he was doing, and I don't want to walk away from this yet. Whatever it is."

"I don't want that either. Let me know as soon as you can," Magnus said.

I pressed my lips to her forehead. "I will. See you soon." I gave her hand one last squeeze, stepped from the apartment, and shifted into my phoenix form.

As the world spread out beneath me, my thoughts wandered. When Bragi called me, and the first few nights I was with him, I expected a betrayal or manipulation every time he opened his mouth.

But as the days turned into weeks, I remembered how good things had been with him. I'd been willing to forgive. Forget.

I'd believed he was sincere when he said he was done lying for love.

Every part of me still believed when he said he loved Magnus, at least in his own way, and even when he said he'd missed me.

But a lie like the one he'd told... Watching Magnus mourn devoured me, and I couldn't feel it. I'd only just started to fall for her.

For Bragi to feel her grief and to know her as well as he did and still actively deceive her...

He was still the man who would do anything for obsession, including hurt said obsession.

I flew for hours without any resolution or satisfaction, so I returned to the city to find a hotel. Every place I walked into refused to let me check in without ID and a credit card.

How long had I been hiding from the world?

I finally found a motel with maybe two dozen rooms, all strung along the length of the parking lot, that let me pay cash and didn't question when I said *I left my ID at home*. It didn't matter that there were no amenities. The place was clean, simple, and didn't contain anything that reminded me of Bragi.

The mattress buckled a little in the middle when I laid on it, but it would do. I searched the patterns in the ceiling, looking for hidden images. Answers.

One of the shapes looked a little like a leopard, but there were no more solutions up there than in my head.

I'd need to go back to my old life soon. But could I? The amount of time I'd known Magnus was a drop in eternity, but I couldn't walk away from her.

She was fighting a war, though. She was on the front line. A soldier, regardless of how much she resented her past. And having Dahlia back didn't mean she would stop trying to balance the world.

Especially not if Vidar was hunting her, but even when he was gone, even if she was personally safe, she'd still fight.

I couldn't sit on the sidelines and do nothing.

Why not? I'd never had a problem with it before. Was I considering throwing away a lifetime of neutrality for a woman I'd just met?

Yes.

When did I lose my mind?

Was it when I saw the redhead from my dreams, broken and near death in Bragi's bed?

No.

Was it the first time I saw her with her healed wings? The first time Magnus and I fucked? That moment when she realized she had all her power back? The dozens of conversations we'd had about our favorite books?

It was none of those, and all of those.

And in the end it didn't matter when it had

happened, because it had. I was willing to fight with her. For her.

I was willing to rewrite my life to be a part of hers, and that was more terrifying than wondering if the next time I died would be the one time I didn't come back.

CHAPTER 21

MAGNUS

I didn't think I'd have this moment. I had my sister back. Nothing else mattered—that needed to be my mantra for the day or I'd crumble in the conflicting emotion.

"I need to burn these clothes." Where did that come from? It didn't matter—the thought was accurate.

Dahlia grabbed my hand. "Change out of them first. It's going to be a long time before I don't have nightmares about you being burned alive."

Same.

She and I headed into my room. I didn't want to let her out of my sight and I suspected she felt the same. I stripped down to nothing and tossed the clothes into the tub. It wasn't that they were bad clothes, but they reminded me I'd been blind when it came to Bragi and they made me question so much.

With a snap of her fingers, Dahlia lit the small pile on fire. Black plumes of smoke flared around us. I waved the fingers on the hand that I wore the ring, and it all swirled into a single column and vanished from the room, sent into the air high above us where it would dissipate without anyone calling the fire department.

The ring worked even better than the last one. "You made this?" I asked Dahlia.

"I did. I'm better at using my dragon magic now, and I know how bummed you were when Artura destroyed the old one, and I just wanted you here so I could give you the new one, and I called and told you so much because I was just hoping you'd pick up, but I knew you wouldn't because you left your phone here, and also because..." She frowned.

I thought you were dead. "I know."

"You should get dressed. Pack. You're coming to stay with us." Cheerful Dahlia was back.

"So I heard." Not that I was complaining. Normally I hated staying more than a day or so at NEON, because it was the Fen-Frey-Dahlia love nest and who needed that?

Besides them, obviously.

But I was safe there. I could keep an eye on Dahlia there. I could make sure this was all real.

I yanked on some of my own clothes. They smelled like my detergent and I'd picked them out myself and they were faded and worn just the way I faded and wore them.

Dahlia perched on the edge of my bed. "Seeing you obliterated broke whatever was holding me back," she said softly. "But it was too late. I was too late. I was a full-on dragon and I couldn't save you."

"I get it. I was just broken for a while. My magic didn't work. I didn't work."

"Is that why you didn't call Frey?"

I was such an idiot. "Bragi told me he'd taken care of it. That he'd called Frey, who was so curious that I'd lived and the two of you hadn't."

"Frey would never..." Dahlia frowned. "Okay, he might."

"See?" I crammed several pairs of leggings into a duffel bag, followed by at least as many tops.

"But not with you. He'd know that you did everything you could."

I finished packing and dropped onto the mattress next to Dahlia. "I was so shattered and if it was hitting me that hard it was going to hit Frey even harder and it wasn't like I could go after anyone until I was healed. *Goddess* I'm such a moron."

I'd believed every line Bragi fed me. Gobbled it up like a scared little puppy. First Vidar, which made me want to vomit when I thought about how much loyalty I'd given him, and then Bragi.

They weren't the same.

But right now it felt like it. "Seriously," I said.

"The only way I could have more toxic taste in men is if I found one who was literally made of toxins."

"You know there has to be a god of poison out there somewhere." Dahlia stood and tugged me to my feet.

I wasn't sure whether to laugh or cry at how real her words were. "We should find him. Hook me up. What's wrong with me?"

"You used up all your luck finding me." Dahlia grinned.

"I might have."

"This isn't your fault."

I sighed. "You're trying to be comforting, but you're not. I made the decision. I made the mistake. I—"

"Shh." Dahlia smooshed a finger to my lips. "I'm not done talking, bitch. Hear me out. You love completely. You give your trust without reservation. You have so much heart—"

"Not anymore." I'd learn to dial that back.

Dahlia slung my big duffel bag over her shoulder. "Don't let Bragi take some of the best parts of you away from you."

Hearing his name hurt so much. "I don't want to go through this again."

"He's not worth being the guy you change for."

My mind was too much of a wreck to do this right now. "I don't want to think about him for now. I want to celebrate that we're both alive."

"Let's go, then." Dahlia pulled me back into the living room and took Fen's hand as well. A moment later we were back at NEON.

The way Frey pulled me into a tight hug squeezed tears from my eyes. "I'm so sorry."

"For what?"

"I thought they were dead. I thought you hated me. I thought..." I didn't have the energy to relive this explanation again.

Fortunately, Dahlia gave him a brief rundown on my behalf. Frey's frown deepened as she talked.

"You're family," Frey said to me when she was done. "No matter what happens, remember that. You're always welcome here. This will always be your home."

Now I was really going to cry. "Thank you."

"We're having a sleepover." Dahlia's enthusiasm was forced, I recognized that after so many years together, but I was grateful for the change of subject. She looked at Fen and Frey. "I'm sleeping over at Magnus's."

Which was ridiculous since I stayed in the apartment next to theirs and Dahlia and I were technically roommates. But I liked the idea of ridiculous. Unstructured.

"We'll order pizza—"

"No." My voice came out more sharply than I intended, carried on a surge of nausea. I was going to

be so pissed if he had ruined pizza for me. "I mean...
Chinese?"

"Get settled upstairs. I've got this." Frey
vanished from the room.

Okay. This was okay. I was okay.

We grabbed sodas from the bar, headed up to the
apartment I stayed in when I was here, and tossed
my stuff in the bedroom. It took us less than five
minutes, but that was enough time for Frey to return
with grease-stained paper bags.

He handed them to Dahlia. "From the vendors
on that street you love in Shanghai."

"Thank you." She gave him a grin and a quick
kiss, and closed him outside in the hallway.

Maybe we should have done that, instead of
staying here. Just gone *someplace*, since I hadn't been
much of anywhere in the last month. Because Bragi
insisted we stay hidden, despite also agreeing with
me that the threat to me was dead.

And I never questioned it. Not even for a second.
How fucked up was this entire situation?

Of course, Vidar *was* looking for me. And Bragi
knew it. And that was the problem.

"How are you? Like right at this moment?"
Dahlia's soft question yanked me out of my thoughts.

I shook my head. "Hungry."

"Easy enough to fix." She unpacked the bags and
laid paper trays, paper-wrapped food, and bowls out

on the kitchen table. There were steamed buns, kabobs, rice dishes, nang bread, and more.

The silence threatened to suck me into an endless cycle of questioning myself. "What did you do while I was gone?" I asked. "You said you left messages, but I'd much rather hear it from you." I tore a piece of meat off a kabob and chewed, to keep myself from rambling.

"There was a lot of crying. Cursing." Dahlia pulled pieces off a bun and ate them. "I swore I felt you a few times. It was so strong, but I convinced myself I was just imagining it."

Like that afternoon in the clearing. "Same."

"At one point, I dragged Frey and Gwydion into the fae realm. But nothing," Dahlia said.

An image flashed in my mind. Bragi stopping therapy early. Rushing us back to his place with an abrupt *it's not safe.* He'd been hiding us from Dahlia? And that was the night I fucked him for the first time.

"Fucking asshole." How much had I missed in his behavior? "I *was* there." It hurt to admit I'd been so close to ending this weeks ago. "I bet you were so close."

"I warded our apartment. You set off the alarm today. I had no idea it was you, just that someone had found the place. And then you were there."

"I was going to hunt them all down." My fury was still there. Finding Dahlia had lessened the grief, but I still wanted TOM to pay. "For putting Vidar in a position to kill you. For creating TOM to begin with. For... I didn't care. I wanted the board to suffer." Apparently I was talking after all.

Dahlia nodded. "Same. He's still out there, and there has to be a reason he hasn't come after Fen yet."

I was so over trying to figure out why the gods made the decisions they did. "Every time we try to out think Vidar, we get fucked. We don't even know how he made each of us think we'd watched the other die..." The answer came to me as I spoke, and it was so obvious it hurt to know we hadn't seen it sooner. "Yes, I do."

"Minato." Dahlia's eyes grew wide.

I nodded. "Minato." The potential Dahlia and I had been hunting when we decided we were tired of killing people on TOM's behalf. The woman we'd secured safe haven for at NEON, who turned out to be a god of dreams.

Minato fed off them, and she could see them and create them as well. And she'd already helped Vidar catch Dahlia once, to try to get information from her before killing her. They hadn't realized at the time that Dahlia was becoming a dragon, and that made the whole *killing* thing difficult.

"Can you find her?" I asked.

Dahlia had the ability to locate magical beings,

including those with just the potential for it. She shook her head. "I couldn't even find you."

"You didn't know you were supposed to be looking, and you almost found me regardless." This was a next step. I knew it was. "Bragi worked hard to keep you from locating me and you almost did anyway. And you have the program you wrote to help."

Determination spread across Dahlia's face. "You're right. We'll find her. We'll start with her, and go from there."

Silence settled into the room as we ate. The ache in my heart grew until it was a throbbing pulse I couldn't ignore, until my limbs just stopped. Until I stopped.

Dahlia put down her food, crawled to me, and wrapped me in a tight hug. "It's all right."

"It will be." My throat was raw. "I'm so glad I have you back. And I needed to know Bragi was a piece of shit, so it's not like I lost anything."

"But it still hurts."

It really did.

CHAPTER 22

NICODEMUS

It took me less than a day before I needed to see Magnus again. In such a short time, she'd become such a huge part of my life.

I was trying to ignore how much I missed Bragi.

She was staying above a nightclub, so it made sense to go back at night, when they were open. I walked into NEON, and a fascinating blend of old and new. Ancient, hand-crafted furniture, hard-wood, and supple leather on the benches and seats. It was all mixed with neon lights and modern music.

I didn't expect to see a familiar face, especially not dancing on stage. I paused near the back of the room to watch Dahlia move in a way that seduced the crowded room.

Would the lust in here drive Bragi mad, or would he embrace it?

"She's stunning isn't she?" A low, smooth voice came from my right.

The dancer was attractive enough, but I was infatuated with someone else. "I prefer redheads." One in particular. "I'm looking for one of the owners."

"A specific one, or is it more of a general request?"

I knew Fen, but I was fine with speaking to either. "More of a general request."

"It's not every day a sexy man walks in here looking for me," he said. His words were flirty, but his posture and tone were guarded.

I doubted that. "It's not?"

"Not without knowing my name. I'm Freyr."

"Nicodemus."

His smile turned genuine and he startled me when he pulled me into a hug. "You saved Magnus. And it's Frey, please."

"Nico. How is she?"

"I'll let you ask her that. I suspect she'll give you a different answer than she'll give me. This way." Frey turned away.

I followed him to the back of a club, down a long hallway, and up a flight of stairs. The instant we stepped onto the second floor, the noise behind us vanished, and something that looked a lot more like the inside of an apartment complex appeared.

It was a similar magic to Bragi's, taking us someplace new when we walked through a doorway.

None of the doors were numbered, or labeled in any way, but Frey went directly up to one and knocked.

It creaked open, but not enough for me to see who was inside.

"You have company." Frey's voice was instantly kind and soothing.

"Who?" Magnus asked.

He stepped back. "See for yourself."

The door opened wider, and Magnus appeared. When she saw me, a smile spread across her face, and the dullness in her eyes vanished in a wash of bright green. This demure creature wasn't the same woman I remembered walking into the library and telling me she wanted to fuck, but she was just as compelling.

"Are you okay to talk?" Frey asked her.

She nodded. "Thank you. We're good. Do you want to come in, Nico?"

I did. I stepped into the apartment, and let her close the door behind me. The instant she faced me again, I cradled her face in my hands and kissed her softly.

Her whimper ended in a sigh and when she kissed back, my heart soared. This wasn't a lust-filled snog, but it was full of desperation. She dug her fingers into my arms, clinging to me. Not that I could let her go. She tasted delicate and fierce, and felt like security and risk, and I needed her close, or I'd drown.

When we finally broke the kiss, we didn't pull apart. I pressed my forehead to Magnus's and lingered in the need that flowed between us.

I finally found my voice. "How are you?"

She tilted her head up to brush her lips over mine, and stepped back. "Before I answer, promise me we won't talk about him."

"I promise. I'm not here for him, I'm here for you. To check on you. To talk about you." And to ignore that part of me understood exactly why Bragi did what he did. It was a teensy part of me, but it was there.

Magnus sighed. "In that case, I'm surviving. I'm home again, and it feels like it, but I can't forget... anything. I keep expecting to wake up and find out it's not real, but I don't know how much of the last few days or weeks I think will vanish."

"I'm sorry." I didn't know what else to say.

"Me too. Can we talk about something else?"

"Anything. You name it."

A hint of mischief slipped onto her face. "You don't mean *anything*."

"I do." At least until she proved otherwise, but my curiosity had blossomed.

"Captain Marvel?" She asked.

I should have known she'd be a fan of the classics. "Mar-Vell? Walter Lawson?"

"Carol Danvers?" Magnus countered. "Wait. You're talking early days. I bet it was so amazing to watch comics come to life back then. Were any of those comic guys gods?"

"Probably. But the ones I knew tended to be nice. And mortal."

Magnus laughed. It was hesitant, but it was definitely a laugh and it was glorious. "Wait. That means you knew the original comic artists."

Was I going to try to impress her with what I'd considered just another chapter of my life up until now? Without question. "I lived in an artist commune with Jack Curtiss."

"Who?" She looked at me blankly. "You'd say that like it should mean something."

I sifted through my memories. Gods weren't the only artists who adopted new names as time went on—mortals just had shorter spans between the name changes. "He changed his name to Jack Kirby at some point."

"No. Shit. Are you serious? You're serious. You lived on a commune with Jack Kirby? I bet that was amazing."

It was whatever it needed to be to get more of that awe and enthusiasm from her. But I had enjoyed it. "It was. Humans tend to be far more imaginative than gods, because they don't assume they know it all."

"You knew all the best people."

I lifted her chin and met her gaze. "I still do."

Her blush was pretty and unexpected, and her smile was worth more than the most sought after art or gems.

Inspiration struck. "Do you want to get out of here?"

"I really really do," she said.

"And you can fly?" I was pretty certain, but it was polite to confirm.

She nodded. "Yes."

"Let's fly."

Magnus took us upstairs rather than down, to a rooftop that looked out over Chicago at about fifty stories rather than the three or four that I expected.

"This isn't the same building we were in," Magnus said. "Just in case you ever land on the roof here and wonder why the doors don't go where you thought."

I was probably more familiar with that than she was. "I'll keep that in mind. Do you want to follow me?"

Magnus summoned her wings in response, and they were still one of the most amazing sights I'd ever witnessed. I shifted into a phoenix.

Her gasp drew my attention, and I perched on a nearby pipe to see her.

"So gorgeous." She reached out her hand then dropped it before touching me.

I wanted to preen, but I settled for spreading my wings to give her a better look.

"Okay, I'll save my awe. Let's go. I'm following you," Magnus said.

We took to the sky. The location I had in mind was probably a ninety-minute flight, but after my trip yesterday, I remembered how much I loved the wind in my feathers, and I suspected she needed some of the same freedom right now.

We stayed high enough to avoid buildings, but low enough to stay out of flight paths, and cut a straight but casual line through the night sky. Our destination was near the state line, along the river. A rocky outcrop in the middle of the forest that over-looked a short waterfall and a small pond.

"It's beautiful." Awe filled Magnus's voice.

I couldn't take my eyes off her long enough to appreciate our surroundings. "You really are."

She laughed and faced me. "You're not going to win me over that way. If all it took was pretty words, I'd have—" Her smile vanished, and her amusement ended in a sad huff.

I'd have stayed with Bragi. "I know. Me too."

"I was surprised to see you today." She sank to the ground and pulled her knees to her chest. "Happy. But surprised."

"I said I'd be back."

"I guess I'm struggling with what to believe."

At least she wasn't questioning the rest of my honesty. "I'll always come for you." Because I was infatuated. Obsessed. In love. I wasn't sure right now was the time to tell her that, but I would, and once she'd heard it, I'd be free to shout it from the rooftops as well.

"What if you die?"

While I understood that was an obstacle to a lot of people, I didn't see why it mattered for me. "You know where to find me when that happens. And I'll come back. It's what I do."

She didn't need to know I'd reach a point one day where I wouldn't. Our history said that we had a life or two of forgetting our past before our future was snuffed out forever, and if I believed that, I had many lives ahead of me still.

CHAPTER 23
MAGNUS

I'd used Nico more than once to ignore how I felt about Bragi. Was I about to do it again?

No. While I didn't love Nico, not yet, the potential was there. I adored him, and he was certainly more than a friend. He'd not only been there for me, but I enjoyed spending time with him.

Once I got him to stop looking at me through rose colored lenses, we'd be even better together.

"How've you been?" Nico asked.

Not the most inventive opener for a conversation, but I didn't know what to say either, and I'd been trained in making small talk. "It's only been a day."

"Ah, but what a day, am I right?" A strain ran through his amused tone.

"You are. You are very correct." I settled on a rock that had enough of a flat surface for sitting, and tucked my knees to one side. "There are these brief, fleeting seconds, nothing more than a heartbeat, where it feels like normal. I forget that for the last month, I thought Dahlia was dead, and for that little blink in time..." I didn't mean to tell him all of that.

"For that little blink in time, it's like the hurt vanishes." Nico finished the thought I hadn't dared speak aloud.

It didn't sound any better when someone else said it. "Is that bad?"

He shook his head. "It's not bad at all. It's reasonable. The dreams, the grief, and everything you went through... None of it was easy."

"Whatever doesn't kill you leaves a lot of scars and some unhealthy coping mechanisms. Am I right?" My laugh was strained.

Nico winced. "I so desperately want to tell you that you're not right, but I see no flaw in your words."

"But you don't usually, do you?" Was I about to turn this into an argument? No, but I did need to know what kind of ideal he saw when he looked at me, and why. "Why did you heal me? That first day, before you knew me, when I was just the unconscious woman in Bragi's bed, and you had no idea who I was. Why did you heal me?"

Nico frowned.

Please don't let this be the moment he starts lying to me.

"You needed the help," he said.

That didn't sound like much of a story. "So you do this all the time? Find people who need help, shed a few tears, and heal them?"

"I haven't done it more than a century."

All righty then. How did I want to drag this out of him? I could stay silent and see what spilled out of his mouth when he was nervous, or I could manipulate the conversation so he thought he was the one controlling its direction, and he gave me the information indirectly.

But all I wanted was the truth, and I wanted him to know that was what he was telling me. "Why not?" I asked.

"It takes a lot to make me cry. *A lot.* Like the pain of a dying Valkyrie who's just watched her sister be consumed by flame."

At his words, my breath lodged in my chest, and I clenched my fist until I could breathe again. "In other words, Bragi shared my feelings with you, it was potent enough to draw a tear, and you stuck around after that just because?" I was missing something.

"Something like that."

I shook my head. "No. I don't want an approximation. Tell me exactly how it was."

"I will. I will tell you the whole story, but I have a request."

"I don't negotiate around lies." Not with people I cared about.

Nico paced in front of me. "This is all the truth, but I have a good idea of how the beginning of the story sounds, and I ask that you listen until the end. It won't be a long story, but the details are important."

"All right. Tell me."

Nico sighed. "When Br— he and I were together, more than a century ago, I had a series of dreams. About a Valkyrie with auburn hair and a spitfire personality and so much heart it almost destroyed her."

My breath caught again. It was obvious he thought he was talking about me. "Okay?"

"The dreams were so potent, Bragi felt them as if my feelings for my dream Valkyrie were real. I shared the vision with him. We became convinced that she must exist. That everyone was wrong who thought Kirby was the only remaining Valkyrie."

Nico didn't look at me, preferring instead, apparently, to watch his toes trace patterns in the dirt. "She became an obsession. I was convinced she was meant to be ours," he said. "And when I finally admitted that searching for her was consuming me in a dangerous way, it hurt as if I'd lost her. As if I'd watched her die."

A stiff breeze sliced around me, and I hugged

myself to stave off the shivers. "So when you saw me in Bragi's bed..."

"You were her, and I couldn't lose you again." He raked shaky fingers through his hair.

And that was why it felt so often like he had me on a pedestal. He was comparing me to a dream woman—an ideal I could never hope to meet. "I'm not her. I'm not a dream. I'm a real person, with flaws and imperfections."

"I know." Nico looked at me. "I've realized that over the last month. The night Bragi called me, I stayed because you were my dream come to life. But the first time I talked to you, it started to dawn on me you are so much more."

He knelt in front of me on the dirt, putting him at my eye-level. "That's the important part of this story. Not what I thought then, but how I feel now. I haven't been falling for a dream, I've been falling for you. For Magnus." He grasped my fingertips. "I'm here for you, not for a flimsy vision who never really existed."

I had no idea how to respond to that. No one had ever said something so beautiful to me. "Flaws and all?"

"Flaws and all." Nico leaned in and kissed me on the forehead, the tip of the nose, and finally on the lips.

This wasn't the same kind of furious intensity I'd shared with Nico before. It wasn't desperation fueled by a need to escape. Rather, I wanted to experience every touch.

His light kisses, the way he slipped my shirt over my head with tenderness, made me think he wanted to savor this as much as I did.

With my top gone, he glided his fingers along my neck, to my collarbone, and down my breastbone.

I wanted to experience both halves of this exploration. When I tugged at the hem of his shirt, he stripped it off and tossed it next to mine. I traced the definition of muscle in his chest, memorizing each line and bulge, and pausing to tease his nipples with my thumb.

Nico reached behind me, and with a single twist, unhooked the snaps on my bra. When he pulled the lingerie away, my nipples perked to life, hard as diamonds thanks to the chill and my desire. He cupped both breasts, and lowered his head to suck on one nipple. He lavished it with attention for several minutes, much to my delight, before moving to the other.

And when he raised his head, he sought out my mouth with his in a hungry, drawn-out kiss.

This was incredible. The slow burn. The anticipation. His kind touch.

It was enough to make me think I could forget Bragi.

Nico pressed his body to mine, and the intensity flowing between us swelled as much as his erection where it dug into my hip. I wanted to feel all of him, so I fumbled with his belt. His zipper. And I finally shoved the rest of his clothes to the ground.

He returned the favor, stripping me down to nothing. He teased a hand along my inner thighs and over my slit, never penetrating me.

My pulse roared in my ears, and I was damp and eager. But I wanted this to last. It was part of now, and also linked to the better parts of what came before. It helped me forget the bad and focus on the good.

Then again, whenever I was with Nico, it was easier to ignore the noise of the world.

Nico pulled me into him as the chill of the night rushed around us, and my body molded to his as if our forms were made to fit together. He was warmer than he should be. Just enough that I felt the breeze on my back, but he kept me from shivering. With my palm on his chest, I felt every beat of his heart thrum into me.

This was incredible, and we'd barely gotten our clothes off. As incredible as flying to a remote, rocky hilltop and fucking a phoenix would be.

Teenage me would be so jealous. When I was at TOM I thought I knew it all. I'd had no idea.

"Magnus."

Vidar's familiar voice was ice racing through my veins and settling in my stomach. I swallowed back a retch when he stepped from nowhere and stopped about a meter away from us. "It's been too long since I saw you like this. We should do it again sometime."

Thoughts of sex were forgotten. My fury soared and I was charging him before he finished talking, in full and summoned Valkyrie armor. The great thing about this magic was that it hid my nakedness. My weapons were in my hands with minimal thought, and I drove my sword toward Vidar's gut.

He was already gone, teleported to a different part of the clearing.

But I'd expected that.

"Oh, red. You should've stayed with Bragi." Vidar looked unfazed as I lunged again, ready to lop off his head if he didn't move.

He did. Big shock. "This is going to hurt you and Dahlia a lot more than it hurts me," Vidar said.

I was already swooping in for my next attack, unwilling to let him pause for breath for even a heartbeat, and willing to shred him with my bare hands if that was what it took to make him suffer.

CHAPTER 24
NICODEMUS

While I didn't know all of the gods, I recognized Vidar from the few times I'd seen him talking to Bragi. Regardless, Vidar was a threat to Magnus, and I didn't hesitate to join the fight. My human form couldn't do much besides throw punches and heal, but my phoenix had a wide array of capabilities.

The instant Magnus summoned her armor, I was a bird. After nearly a month of sparring with her, I had a good idea of how she thought in a fight. All I needed to do was stay out of her way, and distract Vidar.

Her strength was melee based, so she needed to get close to Vidar while he was summoning things like fireballs. So I darted in, pecking to distract him, then soared out of the way for her to do the real damage.

Vidar knocked Magnus back, and blinked out of view, reappearing farther away. I swooped in without hesitation, claws extended and slicing at his face and hands. Like so many immortals, he healed quickly from normal attacks, but mine carried magical fire, and lingered longer.

My goal wasn't my own damage, but to buy Magnus time to do what she needed to.

As I flew at Vidar's neck, he whirled and knocked me back with a growl. "I know you. You're Bragi's pet."

I didn't say a lot in this form, even in a fight, and once upon a time the words would've provoked my anger. At this moment, they didn't matter.

Vidar flung a series of fireballs at Magnus. Fire was my element, more than most. I snuffed them out in midair and drew the dissipating energy into me. The power added to my own, making my cuts more potent. But I was saving most of the energy in reserve. For a single attack.

While I pecked at Vidar's shoulder, Magnus did the real damage, and she was glorious to watch. She never hesitated to strike and slice, moving fluidly with her own defenses and offenses in place. It was clear why she'd been chosen as one of the new Valkyrie.

She wove through the battlefield with targeted precision, slicing Vidar with her sword. Blocking flung lightning. Familiar with the way Vidar moved and ready each time he blinked out of sight.

The longer this went on though, the more likely someone would slip. If it was Vidar, fantastic. If it was Magnus or me, we were fucked.

I sent a rapid-fire barrage of mini-fireballs in Vidar's direction. None of them would harm him, but the quantity was high enough to distract him for a few seconds.

I landed behind Magnus, taking human form for a heartbeat, and kissed her on the cheek. "Find me. Soon."

"Wait. What?" She darted toward Vidar again, but concern rang in her voice.

I flew between them, growing in size, and wrapped my wings—my entire body—around Vidar. We were more or less one now, and I knocked us both away from Magnus. Holding on for all I was worth, I increased the core temperature of my body.

It rose into the hundreds of degrees Celsius. Too hot for any human to survive. Scorching enough to combust most things. The heat was contained to us, and his clothing was on fire. His skin.

His screams tore through the night. This wouldn't destroy him, but it would incapacitate him for a while. Give Magnus time to get away.

We were so close now. He should be almost—

CHAPTER 25

MAGNUS

For the second time in as many months, I watched helpless and horrified as someone I cared about was consumed in flame with, and thanks to, Vidar.

And then it was over. The world was silent, and both god and phoenix were gone.

Find me. Nico's words echoed in my thoughts as I stood in the middle of the new clearing, surrounded by destruction and not much else.

This wasn't happening.

Not again.

"*Fuuuuuck,*" I screamed into the night.

Find me.

I swore I could still hear his voice on the breeze. I didn't have the same connection to him as Dahlia, but I could see one forming. The potential for a centuries-long bond was there, and I wasn't going to sit around and just believe that it was over, like I had with Dahlia.

Speaking of, I pulled my phone from my back pocket of the pile of clothes still dropped by a nearby rock. Should I laugh or cry that those were still intact? I should just be crying. Sobbing at what happened.

The feeling wasn't there. I was removed from my grief, like a portion of me had been numbed and cut out.

Was this what Bragi felt like?

Fuck me for thinking of him now.

Flying home would take too much time and energy, so I called Dahlia. "Can you come get me?"

She didn't ask why, or even hesitate. She was in front of me before I finished getting the question out.

But she did frown when she saw me. "I thought you were with Nico."

"I was." I didn't know how to put this.

"Did he take your clothes and run away?" Dahlia nodded at me.

Oh, fuck. I hadn't gotten dressed yet. "No." I gestured to the pile, then gathered everything into my arms. "We were interrupted."

"I hope you got to finish first." Dahlia's voice was hesitant but teasing.

I gave her a strained laugh. "No."

She took my hand. "Well, come on." A moment

later we were in my apartment again. "Do you want to talk about it?"

I wanted to scream and shout and cry... And I wanted to never feel again. Should I be grateful that I hadn't completely fallen for him yet? That I was close, but not quite there? How fucked up was I to even consider such a question? "I need a shower. I'll talk, you listen."

"Okay." Dahlia followed without argument. As I pulled the glass door in the bathroom shut between us, I saw her sit on the closed toilet seat.

I turned the water on to scorching, because it reminded me of Nico and because I wanted it to burn away everything, and I let it flow over me. Then I needed to scrub away the frustration of the world. The loss. The rage.

"He's gone." I didn't like the way the words tasted, but they didn't rip me apart to say, because Nico's *find me* echoed in my head.

"I figured, seeing how he wasn't there and such," Dahlia said.

I laughed dryly, and grabbed the words I knew would make her tense if I didn't get to the point fast. "Vidar found us. Nico blew both of them up." Okay, that was harder to say.

"Fuck. I'm so sorry."

I let out a shaky breath. "Me too."

"But you know neither of them are gone for good."

"I do." The thought was simultaneously comforting and infuriating.

"What do you need?" Dahlia asked.

A cage for every god in the world. We'd let them out one at a time, after they proved they weren't assholes. Frey and Fen could probably go free first. Gwydion. Min.

The rest had a lot of proving themselves to do.

Other than that… "A way to get drunk, a lot of really crappy junk food, and a way to find Nico again."

Dahlia stood. "Finish your shower. I'll be in the living room with the food, and we'll figure out the plan."

I did what she said. When I joined her on the couch, she already had dinner and drinks laid out on the coffee table.

The cans of Purple Claw were mediocre, the tacos and nachos were far better than they had the right to be, and the company was amazing. Dahlia was just the best. There wasn't much reason to make a plan for finding Nico beyond *go to the place he said he'd be, and wait.*

I should've asked him how long it would take. When Kirby was reincarnated, it had taken decades, sometimes centuries. But Nico made it sound like he'd be back in a day or two.

I went to the small town in Wales that he told me about. The kind of place that had so few residents they noticed all visitors, and closed by nine every night.

The first day I visited, I tried to refrain from overstaying my welcome. I had some coffee, a light lunch, and had Dahlia take me home again.

By the end of the week, she was dropping me off as the bakery opened and not picking me up until things were dark. She offered to stay, but I never let her stick around for more than a few hours. Just because I was killing time, waiting for someone to become un-dead, didn't mean she had to surrender her life.

It was nearly eight on Saturday night, and I was trying to figure out if this was the kind of place that was all buttoned up except for the church on a Sunday, when a flash of red hair caught my eye.

Half the people here were redheads, and as I scanned the crowds, no face was familiar. Until my gaze landed on Nico.

It was him. I stared to make sure, waiting for him to turn one way and then the other, as he ordered a hand pie from a local cart. Fuck me, it was really him.

"Nico," I shouted, and he turned.

He gave me a warm smile and a wave.

I sprinted across the pavement, barely avoiding the other foot traffic, and threw my arms around his neck. His strong, warm body was the perfect match for mine, and I nearly melted into him. I pressed my lips to his in a hungry kiss, sighing with relief when he wrapped his arms around my waist and kissed me back. Everything about this was right. Familiar. Tantalizing.

How fast could we get back to his place? To catch up? I pulled away to ask him.

"I think you've mistaken me for someone else, gorgeous." His thick accent caressed my nerves.

I laughed at the teasing. "Nico."

He shook his head. "Yes. But I don't know you, love."

My heart shattered. I didn't think it was still capable of that.

But I was done being fate's punching bag. Fuck that. I wasn't letting that asshole Vidar steal someone I cared about ever again. I'd help him remember. I'd get my phoenix back.

BRAGI

When I told Magnus that my empathy didn't work across long distances, I left out one little detail. Though I couldn't influence someone who was far away, like any god, I felt so many of those things that gave me power, around the world. And when I knew what one heart felt like, it stood out from the rest no matter where the owner was.

I felt Nico when he died. The background noise that was his heart vanished, and Magnus's grief soared again. The span since I last felt her sadness was brief enough that this was like picking off a scab and it bleeding freely.

A few days later, Nico was back, but his emotions were different. Like switching brands of strawberry ice cream. But I expected that from his rebirth. I wanted to go to Magnus. To comfort her. To point her in the right direction. To *see*.

None of that would be welcome.

I knew the instant Magnus found Nico again. Her joy. Her relief. Her adoration.

His confusion.

Followed by hers. An intense hurt, mixed with a lack of understanding.

Not as potent as her grief, but still painful.

And then I didn't feel anything. Not from Magnus, or Nico. Not from a single soul.

All of the emotion, all of the background noise, was gone. My empathy was gone. I had just lost access to one of my senses, the same as if I could to longer taste or touch.

I was left alone with my own thoughts and heart, and the pain of hearing myself was nearly unbearable.

WHILE EACH BOOK ends on its own cliffhanger, the entire series will offer an HEA for both sisters, Magnus and Dahlia.

The story, the love, the loss, the destruction, and the salvation, continue in ANNIHILATION.